Get Your
Coventry Romances
Home Subscription NOW

And Get These
4 Best-Selling Novels
FREE:

LACEY
by Claudette Williams

THE ROMANTIC WIDOW
by Mollie Chappell

HELENE
by Leonora Blythe

THE HEARTBREAK TRIANGLE
by Nora Hampton

The Smithfield Bargain

Rachelle Edwards

FAWCETT COVENTRY • NEW YORK

THE SMITHFIELD BARGAIN

This book contains the complete text of the original hardcover
edition.

Published by Fawcett Coventry Books, a unit of CBS
Publications, the Consumer Publishing Division of CBS Inc.,
by arrangement with Robert Hale Limited.

ISBN: 0-449-50203-1

Printed in the United States of America

First Fawcett Coventry printing: August 1981

10 9 8 7 6 5 4 3 2 1

The Smithfield Bargain

ONE

Life in a country house such as Hetherington Howard was normally peaceful and uneventful with only the occasional visitor to excite the lives of the servants and inhabitants alike, although, due to the chronic invalidism of the mistress of Hetherington Howard, visitors were rare.

On one bright spring day in the first year of the nineteenth century it was apparently much as usual. The son of the house, Edgar Beaumont, dressed immaculately in a riding-coat and nankeen breeches, his hessian boots shining like glass, was astride his hack inspecting the far reaches of his father's

estate, while George Beaumont himself pe-
rused the accounts presented by his land
steward.

The weather was unseasonably clement
and the younger children were struggling
with their lessons in the schoolroom while
casting longing looks outside at frequent
intervals, much to the annoyance of their
governess. The eldest girl, Georgia, as with
most females of marriageable age was suf-
fering the pangs of first love, which was
proving to be a far from joyful affair. Mrs.
Beaumont, herself, after having dutifully
produced several children, then took to her
sick-bed, from which she contrived to run
her home and everyone who lived within
it, and managed it with remarkable skill
despite her apparent disabilities.

However, on this particular day looks
were very deceiving. The sound of raised
voices within Mrs. Beaumont's private
sitting-room was audible beyond the closed
doors, exciting the interest of all who could
hear. Outside the sitting-room, in the corridor, two maid-servants huddled together,
giggling as they pressed their ears to the
door. Their many pressing chores were
forgotten.

"Wouldn't like to be Miss Haygarth," commented one, her eyes bright with pleasure and excitement, which belied the sympathy in her tone.

"I wouldn't be so hasty as to pity 'er," the other one rejoined. "Miss Haygarth can be just as sharp when she pleases and could be the one to put Mrs. Beaumont in 'er place."

"She wouldn't dare!"

Giggling again they listened in earnest once more until a step behind them made them start.

"Just what do you think you are doing?" demanded the butler, eyeing both maidservants sternly.

Both girls attempted to stammer out an excuse but contrived only to be incoherent.

"Go about your duties immediately, or I shall be obliged to inform Mrs. Kenworthy of your misdemeanour."

The threat of being censured by the tyrannical housekeeper was enough to send them scuttling away. The butler watched them go and then, pausing only to ascertain that the footman attendant in the hall below was occupied, pressed his own ear to the door.

"The worst part of the entire affair is that

it is a flagrant breach of my trust, Miss Haygarth," Mrs. Beaumont could be heard to say in a hurt yet strident tone of voice. "I looked to you for unimpeachable behaviour."

She was reclining on a day-bed. Her dun-coloured crushed taffeta gown did nothing to heighten the colour of her cheeks, but her anger certainly did. Her greying hair was imprisoned in a cap decorated by lace lappets which fluttered to underline the woman's anger. With one hand she clutched a shawl to her breast, the other a vinaigrette which she frequently felt the need to administer to herself.

"I did not betray your trust, Mrs. Beaumont," the recipient of the wrath protested.

Annabel Haygarth was a slightly built girl of no great beauty. However, wearing a gown of grey gingham—considered suitable for a paid companion—she appeared misleadingly mousy, until the light caught her brown curls and turned them to gold, or some emotion enlivened her brown eyes. Emotion certainly gave them depth at that moment, for her inner feelings were being dangerously repressed.

She wrung her hands in anguish. "Please,

Mrs. Beaumont, you are entirely mistaken, I assure you."

Mrs. Beaumont sat upright, remarkably alert. "Mistaken am I? My eldest son declared to me not an hour ago his intention of marrying my own paid companion. You brazen hussy! How dare you stand before me and plead innocence? You have put him up to this!"

Annabel stepped back apace. "Mrs. Beaumont . . . ! I gave him no reason to hope . . ."

The woman's face contorted with fury. "You gave him no reason . . . Oh, I see now you are a scheming baggage determined to leg-shackle yourself to the son of a gentleman. Oh, if it were not for my good nature I should have seen through your scheming ways right from the beginning. Such a conciliatory air, so biddable . . ."

"Mrs. Beaumont . . ."

"And all the time you were scheming to seduce my son!"

Annabel's eyes opened wide with horror. For a moment she was speechless with the shock Mrs. Beaumont's words had caused her, but no longer did she attempt to pacify the woman whose every whim she had sought to satisfy for six months. Colour flared in her cheeks and her eyes sparkled with a fury which matched the other woman's. At that moment she looked quite beautiful although there was no one present to note it.

"Seduce him! You must be mad! Whatever makes you believe I would set my sights on a milksop like Mr. Edgar? For love I would endure the direst poverty, but not for the greatest fortune would I suffer being married into this family."

Mrs. Beaumont gasped now at the unexpectedness of her companion's anger. Indeed, no one had ever spoken to her in such a manner before.

"How dare you speak to me so disrespectfully? I have seen with my own eyes the way you have flirted with him and led him on."

"I have exercised only common civility, and I must reiterate that I did not set my cap at him."

"You cannot be unaware of his eligibility."

"He is not to my fancy!" she retorted. "And whilst we are about it, let me assure you that when Mr. Edgar mentioned marriage to me I refused him immediately. Moreover, if anyone has tried his hand at seduction it is he, and not very skillfully either."

At this latest attack Mrs. Beaumont put out one hand as if to stave off a physical blow. "Miss Haygarth, that is enough!"

But no longer could the girl be silenced so easily. It was as if a dam within her soul had broken, allowing free all pent-up emotion.

"No, it is not enough!" Annabel blazed. "I have been companion to you for six months, and let me say it has been more like six years, pandering to your every whim and imaginary weakness when in truth you are as strong as a horse."

The woman's face turned an unhealthy purple as she sank back into the cushions, pressing her vinaigrette to her nose.

"You will go, Miss Haygarth—now!" she gasped.

Annabel realised she had gone too far, that someone in a position of subservience needs must suppress anger whatever the provocation, and now contrite she stepped forward, but Mrs. Beaumont shrank away even farther.

"Don't touch me. I will not have a creature like you near me or my family. I have done with you. Leave my house. I never wish to set eyes upon you again."

Annabel hesitated only for a moment longer before turning on her heel and rushing to the door. As she reached it Mrs. Beaumont cried, "Do not imagine you can apply to me for a recommendation, you doxy . . ."

Gulping back a sob Annabel fled from the room, almost cannoning into Forbes, the butler. She did not apologise—she was too far beyond rational thought for that. Foremost in her mind was a need to remove herself as far as possible from Mrs. Beaumont. She fled down the curved staircase and out into the blessed freshness of the air.

When she reached the rose garden with its arbours and seats she sank down gratefully on the first one she came to. After a few moments her breathing became less erratic and she brushed away a tear with an impatient hand. It was no use crying now, she recognised; the damage was done.

Oh, it was all too bad that Edgar Beaumont had to try his fledgling wings just now and fall in love with *her*. She could say in all honesty she had done nothing to encourage him, but her gentle indifference had only increased his passion. She had braced herself for a difficult time until Edgar admitted defeat or found a new diversion, but in her wildest dreams she had not imagined he would make this foolish declaration—to his doting mama of all people. Had he been present at that moment Annabel might have been tempted to strangle him, although, in truth, he was an amiable enough young man, favouring his ineffectual papa rather than his overbearing mother.

However, just at the moment Edgar Beaumont was not her prime concern. It was quite obvious that her employment at Hetherington Howard was terminated and would have been even if she had not lost her temper. The fact remained that paid companions should not lose their tempers, even when the situation was so unfair. Annabel knew in her heart she was not suited to such a post but the sad truth was that she was not qualified for anything else, not even to be a governess, which was little better in any event. Demanding children could be just as tiresome as the Mrs. Beaumonts of the world.

With no recommendation from Mrs. Beaumont, Annabel was fully aware that she would find it difficult to secure another post, and the thought of her bleak future was chilling. There was nothing she could do and nowhere to go.

She sat in the arbour for some time, her mind numb, and then after a while something began to permeate her thoughts. Somewhere nearby someone was in as much misery as herself. The sound of sobbing could clearly be heard and Annabel listened for a few moments before pulling her shawl about her. A cool breeze was blowing although she had only just then noticed it. She was without the benefit of bonnet or stout shoes and it was really far too early in the year to be abroad without warm clothing.

Annabel huddled into her shawl and, curious now, she stood up and began to move towards the sound of crying. Finding the source of the noise was an easy task, although she approached cautiously. Hidden behind a budding laurel bush she espied none other than Georgia Beaumont. Her head was bowed and her face hidden in her hands, but her thin shoulders shook convulsively as she sobbed, unaware of being overlooked.

Annabel was immediately diverted from

her own problems at the sight of such heartbreak, for Georgia Beaumont always seemed
the most carefree of the Beaumont brood,
although it appeared they were all somewhat cowed by their mama's overwhelming
personality—even Mr. Beaumont, who had
insisted that Annabel be treated as one of
the family rather than a servant, which, in
truth, she was.

She remained concealed for some few
minutes, uncertain whether to intrude upon
such grief or not. Perhaps the girl would
recover her composure and render interfer-
ence unnecessary. But the weeping did not
cease and Annabel could not conceive what
had caused such heartbreak. Finally she
could bear it no longer.

"Miss Beaumont . . ." she ventured, step-
ping forward. "Miss Beaumont, is anything
amiss?"

The girl looked up, her hazel eyes awash
with tears. She made a hasty attempt to
wipe them away with a lawn handkerchief
which she then concealed in her fist.

"I do beg your pardon, Miss Haygarth, if I
. . . disturbed you. I . . . did not . . . realise
anyone else was nearby."

She looked so distressed Annabel's heart

went out to her even though she was well aware she needed all her compassion for her own situation, which was dire.

Nevertheless she sank down on to the seat at the girl's side. "Miss Beaumont, I cannot help but be aware of your distress. Can I be of any assistance at all?"

"It is so good of you to ask, but no . . . no one can help . . ."

Her chin quivered and the tears began to slide down her cheeks again.

"You are indeed in dire distress, Miss Beaumont. Won't you at least tell me the cause of it?"

Georgia Beaumont clutched the handkerchief in a ball in her fist. "My problems cannot be of interest to anyone but myself, Miss Haygarth."

"Well, I am interested, and although I am certain I can do nothing to help you, at least a sympathetic ear may prove beneficial."

The girl managed to smile at last. "You are full of good sense, Miss Haygarth."

At this pronouncement Annabel strove to hide a wry smile. The truth was that if she had any sense at all she would have been much more conciliatory towards Mrs. Beaumont. Her problems had always been being

far too headstrong, as this morning's out-
burst had proved.

"I dare say you will think me foolish; it is
merely that I am to leave today for a stay
with my godmother in Bath."

Annabel was indeed taken aback. "Are
you unwilling to be parted from your family?" The girl shook her head. "Then why do
you not wish to go?"

Georgia's hand clenched into a fist again.
"My godmother has not set eyes upon me
since I was but a babe, nor I upon her,
although I dare say that does not signify. In
other circumstances I would not mind going,
but the truth is that Mama is sending me to
Bath so that I might meet a nobleman to
marry."

Annabel laughed then. "That is quite a
natural wish, Miss Beaumont. I am only
surprised you take the news so much to
heart. Bath is . . ."

"Bath is so *demodé*, Miss Haygarth. *No
one* of any consequence goes there any more
save elderly invalids. Besides, if the object
of the visit is to marry me off, it is too late; I
have already met the man I wish to marry
right here in Hetherington Howard and

nothing will deflect me from my devotion to *him*."

Once again Annabel was taken aback, for she had heard nothing of it. "Really?"

It was Georgia's turn to smile, dreamily. "Benedict Quinton," she breathed.

"The curate!"

The girl's smile faded. "None other. You too look disapproving although I cannot conceive why. He is quite splendid."

Annabel quickly recovered from her surprise. "I do not doubt it, Miss Beaumont, but it is natural that your family wish for a more . . . brilliant match for one of your standing."

"You are, of course, perfectly correct. Mama will not hear of a match simply because he is a curate with few prospects, but I love him truly and he is devoted to me. With my portion I hardly need wed a wealthy man. We shall not be living in penury."

Annabel put one hand on the girl's arm. "Miss Beaumont, I do understand your feelings now, and I do sympathise with your plight, but surely you can go to Bath in any event. When you return, if your feelings remain constant, your parents are bound to relent."

Georgia twisted her hands together in anguish. "Oh, if only that were so I could endure a month away from Mr. Quinton, and gladly, but even though Papa would as lief give his consent now, Mama has decided I must marry a title, and believe me, Miss Haygarth, nothing will sway her."

"But if you refuse all offers . . ."

"Mama is a woman of considerable will and so, I understand, is Lady Ashley, my godmother. They have decided what my future is to be. I am to be a Smithfield Bargain, Miss Haygarth, an heiress wed to a penniless title."

"That is not necessarily true. You might marry an exceedingly rich aristocrat."

"Tush! No one of any consequence goes to Bath nowadays, and he is like to be old and gouty too."

She buried her head in her hands once again, and despite the outrageous drama of the situation Annabel's heart did go out to the girl. It was totally wrong for a man of worth to be refused out of hand simply because he had not the required wealth or family connections.

"It seems, Miss Beaumont, that we are

both in the devil of a fix," she said with a sigh.

Georgia Beaumont looked up and gazed at her curiously for a moment or two before Annabel added, "I have been dismissed without a recommendation."

"Oh, surely not because of Edgar." Annabel nodded. "He really is a mutton-head. I heard Mama and Papa arguing about it only this morning. Papa said they must ignore the entire affair as it did not signify, but as usual Mama would not heed him. I am so sorry. Filled with my own misery, I did not realise the dire consequences of Edgar's foolish behaviour."

"Why should you? It is, I understand, a hazard faced by all paid companions and governesses, with whom the gentleman of the house, or a son, invariably fall in love and therefore incur the wrath of the mistress. Your brother was ripe for such an infatuation and I was the only one on whom he could pin his callow affections."

"What will you do?" Georgia asked anxiously.

"I do not know as yet. Leave here, of course, and within the next few hours too.

Your mama will not countenance my presence any longer than necessary."

"But, Miss Haygarth, I am not so far removed from the world not to know how difficult it will be for you to obtain another post without recommendation of some description."

"That is the true problem. No one is like to employ me."

"Oh dear, what *shall* you do?"

"I beg of you, Miss Beaumont, not to distress yourself on my account. You have grief enough of your own and I am certain I'll be able to secure employment of some description."

At the reminder of her own situation Georgia Beaumont's eyes grew dim again. "We have both been cast into the depths of despair. If only it were possible for you to come to Bath with me."

"The sentiment is a kind one, but even if it were possible it would solve nothing, for either of us."

"Oh, indeed, I cannot conceive what I was thinking of."

Annabel patted her hand. "We shall both survive this crisis, Miss Beaumont, of that you may be sure."

"Your certainty is to be admired, but I am not so sure I shall. I cannot bear to think of a month without my dearest Benedict, let alone a *lifetime*. I have racked my brain in an effort to think of a solution. Oh, if only I could cut myself into two pieces. One half of me could go to Bath, and the other to Gretna with Mr. Quinton."

Suddenly her entire demeanour brightened. "Miss Haygarth, I have just had the most splendid idea which would serve us both." Annabel looked at her doubtfully. "*You* shall go to Bath in my stead."

Annabel stared at her uncomprehendingly. "Miss Beaumont, what do you mean?"

Georgia Beaumont leaned closer now, talking in a conspiratorial whisper and all the while tugging at Annabel's sleeve in her excitement.

"Do you not see what I am suggesting?"

"I regret I do not."

"You shall go to Bath as Georgia Beaumont and I, under the name of Annabel Haygarth, will go to Gretna with Mr. Quinton. By the time the ruse is discovered it will be too late for anyone to act!"

Annabel jerked away from her in alarm, frightened that the girl had suddenly taken leave of her senses, although she had always seemed, in the past, to be level-headed.

"That is, if I may say so, a ludicrous suggestion!"

"Why? It is perfect. If I do not arrive in Bath, there will be a great hue and cry, and it is like we shall be stopped before we are wed. Utilising my new plan no one will even realise we are gone!"

"I would be denounced as an imposter immediately by all the people who know you."

"Not at all. Lady Ashley has not seen me for sixteen years. She is very like Mama, a semi-invalid. That is why she lives in Bath, so she can take the waters for her health."

"Even so, it would never do."

"I cannot see why not, Miss Haygarth. Generally our descriptions are very much alike. We are of a similar age, as much as makes no difference in any event. You could wear my clothes and I yours. Our colouring is not so different. You are darker, but that is all to the better; dark hair is all the rage now."

Annabel jerked away from her again. "I don't want to be all the rage! Miss Beaumont, you do not know what you suggest. I could not carry off such a masquerade for five and twenty minutes."

The other young lady was quite unconcerned for Annabel's doubts. "You underestimate yourself. My dear Miss Haygarth, if you can contrive to suppress that admirable spirit of yours for six months, I am persuaded you can do *anything*. Recall, it will be for no more than a sennight, until Mr. Quinton and I are married. As soon as that is accomplished I shall dispatch a note to you in Bath and you need continue the pretence no longer."

"And what of me then, Miss Beaumont? Once I am declared an imposter it will hardly be pleasant facing your godmother."

"You will be able to slip away before she is acquainted with the truth. Besides, no one can do anything about it, and you will have earned my eternal gratitude."

Annabel shook her head. "It would not work. I am convinced of it."

Sensing the doubt in Annabel's mind the younger girl pressed on. "Oh, do not imagine you will be leading a hectic social life, for it is not done in Bath; it is one of those places inhabited by elderly invalids. Neither will you be besieged by young men wishing to marry you. Recall it is Bath and anyone paying court to you will be old. In any event, no one will come up to scratch in a *week!*"

"That is the least of my concerns. The entire scheme seems sheer lunacy."

"Indeed it is not," Georgia answered in hurt tones. "And it is not as though you have a pressing engagement elsewhere. You can easily spare a week to be of assistance to me."

This, of course, was true. The reminder was not a welcome one.

"In addition," Miss Beaumont went on, "once I am Mrs. Benedict Quinton, I shall be in a position to write a recommendation to a future employer, claiming quite truthfully, that you were once engaged as a companion to a member of my family."

"Miss Beaumont, I feel . . ."

"You must not trouble your head, Miss Haygarth. I beg of you leave everything to me. You will have little to do until you arrive in Bath and then you need only be yourself."

"But, Miss Beaumont, if I were to agree, the entire venture is so complicated to arrange at such short notice."

"The lack of time can only be our ally in this. I shall suggest to Mama that you travel to the staging-post with me. She is like to agree as it will save the cost of a carriage for you, and no doubt does not believe you merit a conveyance of your own. It could not be better . . .

"Then I shall arrange for Bella, my maid, to take a note to Mr. Quinton. He can meet us at the Black Swan, where you will become Georgia Beaumont and I Annabel Haygarth."

Annabel's head was reeling and she could manage only a fleeting protest. "Miss Beaumont, we must discuss this at more length."

"Fudge! It is a simple matter and we have not the time to discuss anything at length. On the first stage of the journey we will have every opportunity to confer and discuss. Now, I must begin to put my plans into action. We have little time to lose."

The now ebullient Georgia jumped to her feet and rushed off in the direction of the house to complete arrangements for the journey, leaving in the arbour Annabel feeling more than a little bemused after the day's unexpected events.

TWO

It transpired that Mrs. Beaumont was relieved to have gained her daughter's even-
tual agreement for a visit to Bath and
naturally had no suspicion that the obedi-
ent Georgia was plotting to elope. Mrs.
Beaumont was also relieved to be quickly
rid of Annabel too before her son returned
to the house, and agreed that she should be
conveyed as far as the Black Swan in the
carriage which was to take Georgia to Bath.

Annabel packed her belongings in her
cloak-bag and left the house by a side door
in order that Mrs. Beaumont need not set
eyes on her again, and was ensconced in the

carriage when a rather flushed Georgia, accompanied by Bella, her hefty maid, hurriedly left the house. Being 'delicate' Mrs. Beaumont could not brave the air to bid her daughter farewell and as Edgar Beaumont had been spirited to the far side of the estate until Annabel had left, it was, perhaps fortunately, a rather inauspicious departure.

As the carriage set off along the drive Georgia sank back into the squabs and drew a deep sigh of satisfaction, at the same time casting Annabel a conspiratorial smile.

"A note has been delivered to Mr. Quinton," she informed a rather subdued Annabel. "He is to meet us at the Black Swan on the morrow."

Annabel had a sinking feeling in the pit of her stomach. "Are you quite certain, Miss Beaumont. . . . ?"

"Such a lack of spirit is quite unlike you, Miss Haygarth. Do you not welcome the prospect of an adventure? You will find it the greatest diversion, I am sure."

"It is employment, I seek, Miss Beaumont, not a diversion. Only those with ample means can afford to seek diversions of this sort."

Georgia Beaumont dimpled. "Have no fear. As Mrs. Benedict Quinton I shall do my utmost to provide congenial employment for you."

"It is kind of you to be concerned, but I have the gravest misgivings, for I am very much afraid I shall fail to fool Lady Ashley."

"If that is so, it will only be because of your faintheartedness. You know all about our family and can answer any questions put to you. Moreover, you have the manner and address of a gentlewoman."

"I will contrive to do my best, Miss Beaumont, but I am concerned also that you know what you are about to embark upon."

"I am certain she does not, miss." It was the maidservant who spoke for the first time. " 'Tis a terrible thing she's doing."

"Oh, tush, Bella," Georgia answered. "We have been thinking of a way to elope for days. Miss Haygarth's misfortune is the answer to our prayers."

Her eyes were dreamy. "Oh, I do know what I am doing, Miss Haygarth. Mr. Quinton is a most estimable man."

Annabel had to agree that Benedict Quinton was at least no cork-brained dandy, and as unlike Edgar Beaumont as could be imagined. The fact that he had agreed to elope amazed her.

"Does Mr. Quinton realise you may well be disowned by this act?" Annabel asked carefully, "and therefore without the prospect of a fortune."

Georgia smiled happily. "I have told him so a dozen times, but he cares only for me, Miss Haygarth. That is why I love him so."

Satisfied, Annabel relaxed a little more. In truth, despite her misgivings, she knew she had little to lose by the deception and she could not deny that achieving some small revenge over the odious Mrs. Beaumont was not without its satisfaction.

"Within the sennight I shall be Mrs. Quinton," Georgia said with a sigh. "This is all which matters to both of us." She looked earnestly at Annabel. "You *could* affect to be ill, you know."

The carriage rattled over the cobblestones, jerking Annabel into an upright position. "I beg your pardon."

"It would answer all the difficulties you fear you might encounter. When you arrive in Bath contrive to be done up and spend as much time in bed as possible. By the time you recover your spirits, I shall be wed."

For once one of Georgia's notions found favour with Annabel and she began to turn the thought over and over in her mind while the other girl gazed out of the window, her eyes bright with excitement. Some of Annabel's misgivings were beginning to fade and the prospect before her caused a flutter of excitement too. The evil day when she would be forced to seek employment once more was being postponed, and that could only be a good thing.

The Black Swan was a well-known hostelry on the London road, a staging-post for the London Mail. The food and accommodations was known to be excellent and therefore the inn heavily patronised by the nobility. In normal circumstances Annabel would have been hard pressed to afford accommodation at the inn, but on their arrival Georgia Beaumont bespoke a room and a private parlour in the manner born and the landlord did not look at her askance despite her lack of years.

Annabel quickly discovered that the room she was to share for the night with Georgia was a well-appointed one. A fire was lit in the hearth and on inspecting the sheets

Annabel declared them to be both clean and well aired. Georgia, it seemed, could not have cared less what manner of squalor they were to lodge in, for her thoughts were centred on her beloved curate.

Bella uttered dire forecasts from time to time, presumably in the faint hope of changing her mistress's mind, until Georgia told her at last, "Oh, do be silent, Bella. You know full well I cannot abide Friday-faced creatures around me."

"I'm surprised at you, ma'am, for encouraging this madness," the maid said then, addressing herself to Annabel, who immediately felt downcast.

"There is nothing you can say to dissuade me," Georgia declared, demonstrating to Annabel that in her own way Miss Beaumont was as determined a lady as her mama, "so be done with your wailing. How ever long Miss Haygarth delays discovery of my elopement gives us a greater chance of success, and that is all I ask. Unhook my gown, Bella, and then you may dress Miss Haygarth in some of my own clothing."

Both Annabel and the maid looked at her askance and she went on irritably, "Miss Haygarth may as well grow used to being tended by you, Bella, and to wearing my clothes. She can hardly present herself to Lady Ashley wearing her own, suitable as they may be for her purpose."

The clothes were the last thing Annabel was concerned about at that moment. "Miss Beaumont, you cannot think to go to Gretna without the accompaniment of your maid; it would be quite improper."

Georgia laughed then and it was a delightful sound. "It is improper to go at all! But it would not do for you to arrive at Lady Ashley's house without a maid. I shall have Mr. Quinton for company, and, besides, Miss Haygarth, you will need Bella's assistance. She is invaluable, as I know full well."

"But Miss Georgia. . . ." the maid insisted.

"Enough of this argument, woman. In obeying me in this matter you shall still serve me. You *will* accompany Miss Haygarth and I wish to hear no more about it."

Annabel realised then that Georgia Beaumont was more like her formidable mother than anyone yet realised. Even up until that moment she had doubted that the harebrained scheme could succeed, but it now transpired that Georgia had such a strong will it could not fail.

Accompanied by the sullenly silent Bella the two young ladies went down to a supper set out in the private sitting-room. Annabel felt conspicuous in one of Georgia's sprigged muslin gowns, but it was certainly more becoming than any of her own. In fact, she could scarce recognise herself in the mirror when Bella had finished dressing her hair in a confection of ringlets and ribbons.

"La!" Georgia had cried on seeing her, "You are like to cause a sensation in a dull town like Bath."

"I am taking to my sickbed the moment I arrive," Annabel replied, not displeased by the way she looked, for once like a lady of quality rather than an upper servant.

Annabel usually dressed her own hair in a severe style which was meant to make her look older and more sensible and to play down her natural charms, for it was difficult enough for one of her tender age to obtain a post as companion in a family which contained young men, as most did. Now she supposed Mrs. Beaumont would only employ elderly dragons, which served her right. It was what she truly deserved, although Annabel knew she hadn't been deserving of the treatment meted out to her.

The landlord of the inn obsequiously ushered them towards the parlour and as he did so one of his servants came hurrying down the corridor bearing a tray on which were a number of bottles. He gave a perfunctory knock on the door before going into the room which faced the parlour Georgia Beaumont had bespoken. As the door opened a great deal of noise and laughter issued forth. Automatically Annabel turned, curious as to who was making so much noise and she saw that the room was occupied by a number of gentlemen.

That they were gentlemen was plain to see at a glance, for they were dressed in the height of fashion as decreed by Beau Brummell, who, it was rumoured, had the power to make or break a gentleman's sartorial reputation with a mere word. Moreover, it was also said that the Prince of Wales never purchased a suit of clothing without the approval of Brummell.

Each of the gentlemen present on this occasion wore a variation of the dark broadcloth coat, with light-coloured waistcoat, high collar and pristine neck-cloth.

There were a number of bottles already on the table as well as playing-cards, and it appeared that the gaming was well advanced.

As the door opened one of the gentlemen cried, "My pockets are to let, Cranbourne! I can play no more."

The man so addressed merely laughed and gathered up the cards, but as he did so he also became aware of Annabel's interest and his eyes met hers. It was only for the moment, for she quickly looked away again, disturbed by the questioning look he had given her. A moment later after viewing her more carefully through his quizzing glass he let it drop and pushing back his chair he walked across to the door to see better the two young ladies.

Even though Annabel had looked at him for only a few seconds she was aware that he was a fine looking man, although he could not be described as handsome. He was certainly well built, his clothes needed no padding, and was tall with dark curly hair *à la Brutus*.

The landlord ushered Annabel, Miss Beaumont and the maid into the parlour and as he did so Annabel whispered, "We are being quizzed, Miss Beaumont. That gentleman over there is displaying prodigious interest. Perchance he knows you."

Georgia Beaumont cast him only a fleeting glance over her shoulder. "I do not know him. Oh, he is merely a young buck interested in any piece of skirt."

Annabel drew back at such plain speaking from such a gently reared young woman, but when she too glanced back she noted with some relief that the man in question had returned to his cronies and the servant was closing the door.

A cold collation had been provided and Annabel found suddenly that she was hungry, recalling belatedly that she had eaten little all day. Georgia Beaumont, despite her excitement, managed to consume a hearty meal, which surprised her companion somewhat.

"When does Mr. Quinton join us?" she asked when they were replete.

"Tomorrow morning if all goes well," the girl replied, eyeing the plum pie before she held out her plate which Bella obligingly filled. "He will be spreading the word that his aunt in Malvern is ill and he needs must visit her. Poor dear, subterfuge does not become him. I do hope he will contrive. Any error on his part will set Papa off in pursuit."

"I am certain no one can have the faintest notion what you intend to do."

"I trust that you are correct, Miss Haygarth. I have thought on it at length and I cannot find any fault."

"Have you made any plans beyond tomorrow?"

"Oh, indeed. The entire venture is planned to the smallest degree. Mr. Quinton is to hire a fast post-chaise to convey us as quickly as possible to Gretna, where the matrimonial knot will be tied. At the same time you and Bella, Miss Haygarth, are to travel to Bath in my stead. Simple is it not?"

"Fiendishly."

"It will come to grief," Bella predicted darkly, "and I cannot in all conscience agree to aid and abet such a scheme."

"You will do as you are bid," Georgia retorted, "if you wish to remain in my employ once I am a married woman. You certainly cannot expect to remain in Mama's."

Annabel cast the woman a sympathetic look while Georgia became wistful again. "Do you ever think of what would have become of your life if Mama had not dismissed you?"

"I should have been in gainful employment, Miss Beaumont," Annabel replied.

"You cannot pretend to have enjoyed being at Mama's beck and call, the object of her ill humours."

Annabel smiled wryly. "It is of no account now. I have no employment, nor any prospect of it."

"Nonsense. I am honour bound to secure employment for you if it is still what you wish." Annabel gave her a curious look and the girl went on, "There are alternatives, you know."

"Not that I am aware of, Miss Beaumont. If a woman has no personal wealth and no family on which she can throw herself, then she must find employment, or starve."

"Why, Miss Haygarth, with your looks and address you could easily attract a wealthy patron. Everything your heart desires could be yours without having to stoop to being a paid companion."

Annabel was shocked at the suggestion and looked it.

"Miss Beaumont! That is a ludicrous suggestion and out of the question."

Georgia Beaumont was not at all put out. "Well, then, you might attract the attention of some old colonel whilst you are in Bath, who, if you act purposefully enough, is like to make you his wife."

"Miss Beaumont!" Annabel looked equally horrified at this suggestion. "That is almost as bad."

The girl chuckled. "You might consider it better than being employed by ill-tempered ladies who for ever plague you with their whims."

"Hardly," Annabel replied, smiling wryly now. "An ill-tempered spouse could be even more tiresome."

"Even if he conveniently expires and leaves you a rich widow?"

Annabel laughed out loud. "You are for ever funning, Miss Beaumont."

"The truth is, if only you will face it, you cannot afford romantic scruples," Georgia said bluntly, "although it would suit me to make everyone as happy as I am."

Georgia continued to look at her with interest. "You must not make the mistake of selling yourself short just because you are in reduced circumstances. You are not in the ordinary way of Friday-faced crea-

tures who grease the boots of ill-natured
invalids. You are a woman of breeding and
of spirit, Miss Haygarth. The entire household is full of admiration for the way you
scorched Mama with your tongue."

Annabel was not much surprised that
everyone knew of it. "The result proves it
was ill-considered of me."

"If you had not spoken to her so you
might not have been here now, embarking
upon this adventure with me."

"Ordeal," Annabel amended, "and I am
not at all convinced that it is a sane venture, to say the least."

"Even though I am the one with the
most to gain I vow that you will not regret
it."

"I trust that you are correct."

"We'll all regret it," Bella moaned. "Just
see if we don't. 'Tis madness, that's what it
is."

"Tush," was her mistress's rejoinder and
then, "Tell me, Miss Haygarth, how you
came to be forced to become a paid companion, for I am persuaded that is not what you
would really wish to be."

"I shall not pretend that it is, Miss Beaumont, but the sad truth is that I am qualified for nothing else."

"You should not have been put in such an invidious position. I feel that we are equals."

"Thank you, Miss Beaumont," Annabel answered, her voice heavy with irony. "The story is a common one and of little interest."

"On the contrary, I am most interested, and we have time to pass."

Annabel drew a sigh. "My parents were indeed gentlefolk, as you perceived, but my father was a dreamer with little understanding or interest in estate affairs. Coupled with an incompetent land steward he was soon in dun territory and forced to sell his parcel of land to settle his debts. We moved to the city where my father attempted to tutor the children of the middle classes to provide us with a living. Unfortunately, he was not suited to that either, although it did provide for us, but he soon succumbed to an excess of alcohol."

Annabel spoke matter-of-factly, but Georgia Beaumont looked horrified. "Oh, what a shame, Miss Haygarth. It is a sad tale indeed. Where is your mama now?"

"She died three years ago. We contrived to live well enough until then when I realised

I needs must seek my own way in the world, which so far I have managed to do."

Earnestly the girl answered, "You can rely upon me to help you in any way I can. You have had more than your fair share of ill-fortune."

Annabel smiled. "You are very kind."

"I shall always be in your debt, you must know."

Annabel got to her feet. "I beg of you not to think of it as such, and we really should retire to bed now. It has been a tiring day and tomorrow will be even more so, I fear."

Obligingly, Georgia got to her feet. "You are, of course, correct, but I fear I shall not sleep for excitement." As they collected up their reticules and shawls Georgia asked, "Did you never wish to marry, Miss Haygarth?"

"A woman in my position rarely has the opportunity. Certainly none has come my way and I would not for anything encourage a moon-calf such as your brother."

The girl laughed delightedly. "Edgar is a fool and you have too many scruples for your own good. Mama's chuckle-headed too for making an issue of it. When I am married

I must find a husband for you; I see that is the only thing to do."

Annabel again looked horrified. "Oh, no, Miss Beaumont, I beg of you not to think of it. A situation in a respectable household will suffice."

Georgia looked at her in astonishment. "Come now, you must wish to marry in your secret heart. I do not for one moment believe you have no romance or practicability in you."

Annabel was forced to avert her eyes. "Indeed, but not to a gouty old colonel."

Georgia Beaumont laughed delightedly. "What kind of man do you have in mind, Miss Haygarth? I shall do my best to oblige."

Fleetingly and unbidden the memory of the gentleman in the parlour came to her mind before she deliberately put it from her thoughts.

Smiling at the other girl she said gently, "Let us see you happily settled first, Miss Beaumont."

"I always go too fast, but your plight has touched me and I am persuaded Mr. Quinton will wish me to see you settled in one way or another."

So saying she swept out of the room, followed by the faithful Bella. Annabel was beginning to wonder what she had got herself into and sighed deeply before following them from the room.

THREE

Both young women were awake early the following morning, mainly because of an anxiety to be on their way, but also because life at an important staging-inn started early in the day.

From daybreak carriages rumbled in and out of the courtyard and ostlers hurried to take charge of sweating horses, calling out to one another as they did so.

Once again Annabel felt strange and more than a little guilty at being dressed in Georgia's clothes, this time a blue velvet travelling gown which had a matching feathered bonnet and braided pelisse. It had been specially ordered by Mrs. Beaumont for her daughter's visit to Bath and Annabel hated to think what the woman would say if she could see her wearing it instead.

"You're in high feather, there is no doubt of it," Georgia commented as she inspected Annabel carefully.

"I'm full of forebodings."

Georgia turned away to adjust Annabel's shabby spencer which she herself was wearing. "Fudge. You will contrive perfectly well. I have the fullest confidence in your ability, my dear."

When there came a knock on the door. Georgia started and looked momentarily alarmed but then she motioned Bella to answer the summons.

"A gentleman to see Miss Haygarth," the inn servant announced.

Annabel started with fear and Georgia said in a tone which scarcely suppressed her excitement. "It's Mr. Quinton. I told him to ask for Miss Haygarth to allay suspicion in the event inquiries are made." She turned to Bella. "Give the instruction for him to be sent up."

As the servant left to do her bidding Annabel was frighteningly aware that they were approaching the point from which there would be no turning back and she said breathlessly, "There is still time to change your mind, Miss Beaumont."

"Oh, never. Never," the girl vowed.

"Elopement is a drastic step which needs much consideration and I fear you have not thought on it at length."

Georgia Beaumont dimpled. "You must not pretend that it is the elopement which concerns you; you are thinking more of the part which you will have to play."

"Do you blame me for that?"

"Of course not. It must seem alarming, I own, but you must recall that there is no one in Bath who has the least notion what I look like."

Annabel felt she could argue no more and when Benedict Quinton was ushered into the room his betrothed ran to grip his hands.

"Benedict. Oh, Benedict my dear, has your journey been uneventful?"

"Indeed. There have been no problems."

She beamed. "It is a good omen. Well, then, my dear, is everything in readiness?"

The young man looked rather bewildered, which Annabel found understandable. He looked frightened too, perhaps inveigled into the affair much as she had been, against his better judgment.

"Yes, I have a chaise waiting in the court-yard. We must be gone as soon as possible."

"Yes, yes, I can scarcely wait to tie the matrimonial knot, but first let me acquaint you with Miss Haygarth, without whom we should both be cast into the darkest despair."

She led him across the room towards Annabel. The young man took her hand briefly in his. "We are indebted to you, Miss Haygarth."

She was hard pressed to know how to answer; still far from certain she was doing the couple a real service. He was obviously devoted to Georgia Beaumont but he seemed uncertain about the wisdom of the step he was about to take.

Moments later he was addressing Georgia again, "My dear, we must make haste if we are to reach Gretna in three days' time."

"Oh, if only our arrival there was imminent!"

She scooped up her reticule and bandbox before saying to Bella, "Serve Miss Haygarth as you would me."

The woman remained impassive, tight-lipped with disapproval.

Suddenly Annabel darted forward. "Your jewel case, Miss Beaumont, you must not forget it."

Georgia smiled. "The omission was deliberate. You will put them to better use than I, in Bath, and from now onwards you must remember that you are Georgia Beaumont."

Once again Annabel experienced a gnawing uncertainty but before she could voice any of her doubts the other girl crossed the room and took her hand in hers. "Thank you, Annabel, and good luck."

Mr. Quinton took her arm and hurried her from the room as Annabel answered, "Good luck to you, Miss Beaumont."

Left alone Annabel bit her lip in apprehension and then went to the window to watch the couple depart. Moments later a rather red-eyed Bella came panting up the stairs.

"Miss . . . Miss," she gasped, "the carriage is ready and we, too, must leave immediately."

Not accustomed to being served by others Annabel hurried around the room herself to ascertain that all their possessions were safely packed, and then she tied on the feathered bonnet. She was amazed the difference fine clothes made to her appearance and her gaze lingered at the reflection in the mirror.

"Miss . . ." Bella ventured again causing Annabel to move away from the mirror.

Bella took charge of the jewel case and as she did so Annabel murmured, "For both our sakes, Bella, I pray your mistress makes haste to return."

"Aye," the woman agreed dourly.

Annabel lifted the skirt of Georgia's velvet gown and negotiated the stairs carefully. At the bottom the landlord awaited her.

"I trust that all has been to your satisfaction, Miss Beaumont, ma'am."

She was momentarily startled at being confronted so soon by her new position so she could only smile and nod, but it sufficed, for the landlord ushered her into the courtyard. A chaise was waiting there, a postboy holding the harness of one of the horses which was straining to go.

The only other vehicle evident was a splendid curricle, emblazoned with an aristocratic escutcheon, and the ostlers were carefully putting to a team of magnificent greys. Annabel felt bound to stop and admire them.

"You have an important guest, landlord," she commented, automatically leaving her companion's obsequious manner aside and adopting a more haughty one.

"Indeed, ma'am. The Marquis of Cranbourne. He is a frequent visitor. The Black Swan is renowned far and wide for its hospitality among the Quality."

She smiled. "That is something which has impressed itself upon me and you may be certain I shall not hesitate to recommend it."

Georgia had insisted Annabel accept some money to tide her over, so she was able to give the man a substantial vail which he pocketed with alacrity.

"I am indeed gratified, ma'am, and look forward to welcoming you here again before long."

He was about to hand her into the chaise when another departing visitor strolled into the courtyard.

"If you will excuse me, ma'am," the landlord begged, leaving Annabel to her own devices while he scuttled away to escort the

man she had noticed the previous evening
to his curricle.

She was more than a little miffed at the
slight although she could not blame the
innkeeper preferring to grease the boots of
a nobleman rather than a mere Miss Beaumont.

As she turned away the marquis raised
his curly-brimmed beaver in her direction
but she affected not to notice even when he
strolled towards the chaise and inspected it
carefully. When he looked into the carriage
itself Annabel drew down the blinds and
was glad to hear the driver climb onto the
box.

She could not help but draw a sigh of
relief when the inn was left behind. So far
Georgia Beaumont's plan was working well
and she was beginning to feel less tense;
after all the innkeeper had accepted her
quite naturally so there was no reason why
others should not do so too.

The chaise was a well-sprung comforta-
bly appointed carriage and Annabel sank
back, luxuriating in the comfort. In other
circumstances she would have been aboard
the London stage, an uncomfortable enough
experience even if an uncertain future had

not been before her. At least that prospect was now postponed for a while and the next few days would be spent in the kind of luxury she could not deny she enjoyed. The prospect was very welcoming even if it was likely to come to a quick and possibly unpleasant end.

Annabel dozed spasmodically as the chaise rumbled along narrow country lanes which were heavily overhung with dripping trees, for a light drizzle had begun to fall. The horses had been changed several times and, thankfully, this was the last leg of the journey.

Allied with her haste to have the lengthy journey over, there was a considerable reluctance to be in Bath when the masquerade would begin in earnest. It was bound to be a time fraught with stress. She only hoped that Georgia Beaumont was not mistaken when she avowed that her godmother did not know what she looked like. Even if that were so, the pretence was not going to be easy and Annabel had decided she would definitely feign illness for as long as possible, thus keeping herself aloof from both people and events.

The jerking of the chaise, well sprung as it may have been, eventually lulled her into an uneven sleep, but she had initially closed her eyes as a defence against Bella's continuous moaning. Not that the woman was so concerned about Miss Beaumont eloping any more, rather than she had embarked upon the journey without her maid.

Some time later Annabel was jerked out of her uneven sleep by Bella crying, "Oh, do look, miss!"

She opened her eyes and then after a moment followed the direction of Bella's pointing finger. In the valley below the ancient city of Bath was spread before them, with the tower of the Abbey in the centre.

"So, we are almost there at last," Annabel murmured.

The road began to descend steeply into the valley, the horses picking their way carefully over the uneven surface, and once again Annabel began to experience the now familiar feeling of apprehension. The ordeal, for she could think of it as nothing else, was about to begin.

Suddenly the chaise shuddered to a stop, almost catapulting the two passengers forward. Fortunately, they managed to hold

on to the straps and retain both their seats
and their dignity. No further stops were
scheduled before arrival in Bath and they
were still in the middle of the country.
Annabel sat up straight to crane her neck
in order to see what had caused the unexpected delay.

She was just about to call out to the
driver for an explanation when the window
grew dark, shaded by the bulk of a man on
horseback. Alarmed, Annabel shrank back
into the squabs as the door flew open. A
hand appeared with a pistol in it before she
had any chance to recover her surprise and
demand an explanation.

"Yer money, ma'am, and none'll be hurt."

Annabel cried, "Oh," and Bella screamed.

"Hurry now," ordered the highwayman
and even though she was rigid with fear
Annabel could see now that the man had a
muffler covering the bottom half of his face.
Two malevolent eyes were all that could be
seen, apart from a few tufts of greasy hair
beneath a three-cornered hat.

Gentlemen of the Road these scoundrels
termed themselves, but Annabel could see
that there was nothing gentlemanly about
this highwayman.

"I'm in a hurry. Doesn't do to tarry on the high toby," he warned.

"I have no . . . money," Annabel managed to say at last, aware that the driver and postillion were standing at the roadside with their hands in the air.

It passed through her mind that they appeared ridiculous, trembling in their fine livery.

In the ensuing silence the faint sound of hooves could be heard approaching on the road behind them and Annabel felt a stirring of hope, although sensed it was more likely the highwayman would kill them if there was a chance of interruption.

"Yer jewells'll do." He waved the pistol at Bella. "I won't wait much longer."

Annabel could see no alternative but to give him the box, although she hated to think of losing Georgia Beaumont's jewellery so soon.

"You'd best give them to him," she told the abigail. "He is like to kill us and take them anyway."

"Right, miss," the scoundrel agreed, and then to Bella, "Hand them over nice and easy, mother."

"Mother! I'll thank you not to be so facy!" the woman responded.

Suddenly the sound of a shot filled the air, causing Annabel and Bella to cry out in alarm and to shrink back into the squabs. The highwayman lunged forward to take the jewel box, but acting in a purely automatic fashion with no aforethought Annabel pushed them out of reach and, swearing foully, the robber turned his horse and galloped away at full speed.

Hardly daring to believe they were safe and not questioning how it came about Annabel began to climb down from the carriage. However, she discovered that her legs were far from steady. She clung on to the side of the carriage, fighting off faintness. Suddenly, though, she was being supported by a pair of strong arms which lifted her up and deposited her gently inside the carriage again.

"A vinaigrette for your mistress," a voice ordered.

Bella, who always responded well to autocratic commands, hastened to obey, but by then Annabel was well on her way to recovery and pushed it away.

"I am perfectly all right. I am not in the

least vaporish and I would be obliged if you don't fuss."

Aware at last of the presence of a third person she looked around sharply and noticed then the man who was standing at the open carriage door, looking at her with what appeared to be a mixture of concern and amusement. Annabel struggled into a sitting position, straightening both her bonnet and pelisse as she did so.

"Lord Cranbourne. . . ."

He removed his hat in a sweeping manner. "I am honoured by your recognition, ma'am."

She put one hand to her head. "I confess to being totally bewildered. Has that wretched fellow truly gone?"

"He has, ma'am."

"What . . . what happened? The creature rode away . . . there was a shot. . . ."

"It was discharged by me and I regret that it alarmed you."

"*You* caused him to flee," she said in astonishment.

He looked slightly bashful. "I believe so, ma'am. You see, the road lends itself to sudden and spectacular views. It was a fortunate instance that I had a clear view of the holdup as my carriage negotiated one of the previous bends. I was able to approach on foot and fire a shot which, although it missed, at least sent him on his way." He looked suddenly concerned. "I do trust that the scoundrel caused you no harm and stole no valuables."

Annabel shook her head, suddenly aware of his constant surveyance of her.

"No, indeed; your arrival was opportune and we are extremely fortunate that you were close by."

"I am equally glad to have been of service to you, ma'am. Coombe Down is notorious for its tobymen, so it is exceedingly foolhardy to travel this road unprotected."

"With two servants in attendance I would have thought we were sufficiently protected."

Lord Cranbourne gave the two men a scathing look before answering, smiling urbanely, "You can be forgiven the error, ma'am." After giving her a further considering look he added, "May I know the name of the lady whom I have the honour of serving?"

Startled, Annabel almost said her real name, but just at the last moment choked it back although she could not quite give Georgia's. It was Bella who came to her rescue.

"Miss Georgia Beaumont, my lord."

Lord Cranbourne's consideration was definitely disturbing as he repeated, "Miss Georgia Beaumont. And from where do you come, ma'am?"

"Hetherington Howard," she replied, for this at least was broadly true, and she put her slight breathlessness down to her recent fright.

"I know it," he replied.

"You do?" she asked, alarmed anew.

"The Beaumonts are well known among the landowning fraternity, and Hetherington Howard is a fine parcel of land."

Annabel was somewhat relieved to learn that his knowledge was not a first-hand one. She gave him a curious look then.

"Lord Cranbourne, you were at the Black Swan and it seems odd to me that you, in your curricle, should still be behind us. I would have thought you'd be at least a day's journey ahead."

He smiled blandly. "I have made several lengthy stops since the Black Swan."

She needed no further explanation as to why and she watched him disparagingly as he took a gold snuff-box out of his pocket.

After taking a pinch and returning the box to his pocket he looked at her again.

"I assume you are bound for Bath, so I suggest that you allow me to precede you."

"Oh, there is no need for that, Lord Cranbourne!" she protested, anxious to make as unheralded an entrance as was possible. Being escorted by the Marquis of Cranbourne was the last thing desirable in the circumstances.

"Nonsense. It will safeguard the peace of the remainder of your journey. There may well be other malcontents skulking in the trees, ready to pounce on unsuspecting travellers. Where in Bath are you bound?"

This question truly alarmed her, for she had no notion where Miss Beaumont's godmother lived. Again it was the abigail who came to her rescue and Annabel could at last see the virtue of having Georgia's maid with her.

"Lady Ashley's house in Pulteney Street, my lord."

"It is not out of my way," he answered, somewhat magnanimously Annabel thought. "I myself stay in North Parade," adding as he moved away, "Do you stay there for long?"

"Four weeks, Lord Cranbourne."

"Then it is like that we shall meet often."

She could hear him instructing the driver to wait until he had brought up his curricle and on reflection she considered him to be a rather overbearing young man. She recalled also that he must be a hardened gamester and no doubt embraced all the other vices prevalent in high society.

As he drove past the waiting chaise he waved to her and once more she affected not to notice, turning her face away. He was, she thought, the kind of man Edgar Beaumont would probably admire and wish to emulate, and as the chaise jerked into movement at last she made up her mind that she was not going to be charmed into liking the Marquis of Cranbourne, even bearing in mind the debt she owed him.

FOUR

The elegant curricle turned into Pulteney Street just ahead of Annabel's chaise. Driving through Bath she had noted a great number of fashionably attired people strolling about, although she had been more aware of the marquis's unwanted presence just ahead of them.

Arriving at Lady Ashley's house she immediately noted it was a neat one, separated from the road by a row of railings. As the chaise stopped outside Lord Cranbourne raised his hat and, to her relief, drove on. Their drive through Bath had already excited a good deal of interest from those on foot as, no doubt, Lord Cranbourne was well known in the area.

Annabel looked at Bella as the driver put down the steps.

"Miss Beaumont told me that Bath was *demodé,* that no one young or fashionable came here any more."

The maid shook her head in bewilderment. "It doesn't seem so, miss, I must say."

"Not from what I have observed anyway."

A liveried footman flung open the door, but before Annabel could enter a young woman of about seventeen years came running down the stairs, her gold curls escaping their pins. Her eyes, a light, clear, blue, were wide and bright.

"Miss Beaumont! I saw you arrive from Aunt Phoebe's drawing-room window and I couldn't wait to greet you a moment longer. I've been standing there for hours just waiting for you to arrive!"

Annabel was alarmed, but strove to remain calm now that the real testing time had arrived. The streak of pride which had been her undoing now ensured she did not lose her calm. The girl had addressed her as Miss Beaumont, which helped to reassure her a little.

She handed her hat and muff to the footman and then looked at the girl who said, "You are not, of course, acquainted with me as yet. I am Emma Daunty, Lady Ashley's niece. I am to be here for the month too. I have been so looking forward to meeting you, and so has Aunt Phoebe."

Catching a glimpse of herself in the mirror Annabel brushed back a lock of her hair from where it had fallen forward and then said, "I am glad to make your acquaintance, Miss Daunty, but I wasn't aware there was to be another here at this time."

"You may call me Emma, and Aunt Phoebe thought it might be dull here for you with no young people for company."

Annabel smiled, relaxing slightly. "What a nice notion."

"Come," Emma urged, "Aunt Phoebe is waiting. You must be all done up after your journey."

They started up the stairs. Annabel was still feeling very apprehensive and together with her recent ordeal she was certain it would not be difficult to feign illness after the initial meeting with Lady Ashley.

The other girl's eyes shone brightly with excitement. "Tell me how you came to be

escorted by Lord Cranbourne! I could scarce
believe my eyes when I saw it was he."

Annabel looked at her in surprise. "Do
you know him?"

"Everyone does. He is a great friend of
the Prince of Wales and Brummell, not to
mention being the most eligible bachelor in
London. How long have you been acquainted
with him?"

"For about an hour. We met by chance on
the road just outside the town. My chaise
was being held up by a highwayman and
Lord Cranbourne came to the rescue."

Emma Daunty's eyes grew wider and she
clasped her hands together at her breast.
"How famous! Did you fall madly in love
with him on sight?"

Annabel could not help but laugh. "Of
course not. I am very much obliged, naturally. . . ."

At the top of the stairs another footman
threw open double doors and the two young
ladies were admitted to Lady Ashley's
sitting-room. It was a scene with which
Annabel was familiar, the blinds half closed,
no windows open, a fire in the hearth despite the warmth of the afternoon, and a

lady reclining on a day-bed in an attitude of extreme langour.

"Come closer, my dear," the lady urged.

Annabel obligingly approached the day-bed and gave a little curtsy while the countess scrutinised her closely.

After what seemed to be an agonisingly long time, the woman at last spoke. "You are very presentable. Your mama did not exaggerate and I am so pleased your baby curls have grown darker with the passing of time. Fair hair is quite *demodé* now."

Emma Daunty looked downcast and her aunt added quickly, "You are quite charming, my dear. I have no fears for your future."

At close quarters Annabel discovered that Lady Ashley was not quite what she had at first seemed. She was quite unlike Mrs. Beaumont. There was none of the invalid's pallor about her cheeks, and her expression was one of sweetness as opposed to the expected peevishness. She was wearing a négligé of red velvet and her auburn curls peeped out from beneath a lawn cap. She was small and dainty and her demeanour gave the impression she was still young although Annabel knew her to be middle-aged.

"How glad I am to have you here at last, my dear. I can scarce conceive that you are a woman, but indeed you are and much different, I own, to how I imagined you to be. I cannot decide which family you favour most. Your mama's, I fancy."

In other circumstances Annabel would have been amused at being likened to any part of Mrs. Beaumont's family, but she could only allow herself a small smile.

"Did you journey well, my dear?"

"Aunt Phoebe, only listen to what has happened!" Emma said excitedly. "Georgia's carriage was held up by a tobyman, and Lord *Cranbourne* came to her rescue."

Lady Ashley's eyes grew larger. "Is that so?"

Quickly Annabel related the tale and Lady Ashley smiled. "Well, apart from the unfortunate shock to your nerves caused by the encounter with the highwayman, you are already acquainted with one very eligible young man. Your mama will be well pleased, although," she added, frowning slightly, "I cannot conceive what he is doing here in Bath just now."

"Does he not usually visit?"

"Usually he is with the Prince of Wales at his farmhouse in Brighthelmstone at this time of the year. Of course there is that woman in Landsdowne ... but then I believed that affair over. . . ."

Recalling her intention to retire immediately to her sickbed Annabel put one hand to her head. "The memory of the encounter pains me deeply. I am entirely done up by the experience, Lady Ashley, and feel the headache coming on."

The older woman patted her hand. "Of course you must rest, my dear, for as long as you wish. I shall see that your maid is given some laudanum for you. It works wonders. There is a deal of time during which we can enjoy a coze when you feel better. Emma, take Georgia to her room if you please."

Annabel felt little better for being accepted by Lady Ashley as Georgia Beaumont. For one thing Lady Ashley was a much nicer person than she had anticipated, but at least she had not been denounced as a fraud. Not surprising really, as Lady Ashley had not seen her goddaughter since she was two years old. Even so, Annabel had been worried for a while.

"Tell me what Lord Cranbourne said to you—every word," Emma urged as she led the way to Annabel's room.

"I couldn't possibly recall," she replied, much to the girl's surprise, and on reaching the room where Bella was busily setting out Georgia Beaumont's belongings, she added kindly, "Perhaps we, too, can enjoy a coze together when I am recovered from the ordeal. I really am very fatigued."

Emma Daunty dimpled good-naturedly. "I am a chuckle-head to plague you so. It is only that a hundred girls would give anything for a word from Lord Cranbourne, whereas you. . . ."

Annabel smiled too. "I am not impressed by him, Emma. In all truth I detest such men of fashion."

Emma Daunty looked horrified before answering, much to Annabel's amusement. "You really are done up, Georgia. I fancy a day or two of rest and reflection will see you in quite a different mind."

Annabel successfully contrived to remain in her room for the next twenty-four hours, first claiming tiredness as the reason, then a recurrence of her headache, with a fever being kept in reserve should she need to feign illness longer than expected.

She had brought several volumes of poetry with her but not being accustomed to such a leisurely life soon grew tired of reading for long periods, and being confined to her room soon became wearing too.

"I do hope Miss Beaumont and Mr. Quinton succeed soon in being married," she told Bella. "I do not know how long I can continue this pretence."

" 'Tis better than the alternative, miss."

"I have no mind to be launched into Bath society, especially as it seems I might be connected with Lord Cranbourne in everyone's minds. I cannot think of anything more ruinous to the plan than being the object of *on dits*."

"I'm sure you fret unnecessarily," Bella answered. "Miss Georgia and Mr. Quinton were determined to be wed and I am certain they'll contrive as soon as possible."

"I hope you may be correct," Annabel replied in heartfelt tones. "I long to walk out, and yet I dare not."

Surprisingly, Bella said. "It's good in you to help the young couple."

"I hope to help myself too. Without Miss Beaumont's assistance I am unlikely to find a congenial post."

There came a knock on the door and Annabel quickly climbed into bed. Moments later Bella admitted Emma to the room. She had been a frequent visitor and it was obvious that the girl was anxious for Annabel to be well enough to accompany her to the shops and generally be seen around the town.

"How are you feeling today?" she asked in a hushed whisper.

"Much the same," Annabel answered, affecting a languid air.

"Oh, it really is too bad, Georgia. You are missing so much and after journeying so far too. What a disappointment."

"It cannot be helped. Illness is an uninvited visitor."

Emma dimpled then. "It has its advantages I must own. At least your arrival did not go unnoticed."

Annabel gave her a suspicious look. "What . . . do you mean?"

"Since your arrival there has been an increase in the number of Aunt Phoebe's callers, including," she paused, "Lord Cranbourne."

At this news Annabel sat up against the pillows. "Of course," Emma went on nonchalantly, "it was evident he came to see *you* not Aunt Phoebe."

"I cannot conceive why you should assume that is so," Annabel answered quickly. "It is quite like he would visit Lady Ashley."

"They are not greatly acquainted." The girl almost jumped up and down with excitement. "Did you ever see a man so fine looking, Georgia?"

Annabel looked away, alarmed and yet undeniably excited. "I cannot think him handsome."

"And I cannot understand your attitude. Perchance it will change when you are a little more recovered. The indisposition might have made you peevish, for I am convinced it is not natural in you. Aunt Phoebe says that if you are no more improved by the afternoon she will summon her physician to attend you."

This was the one eventuality that Annabel had feared, and she hastened to say. "Oh, please entreat her not to trouble, Emma. There is no need, I assure you."

"From the paleness of your cheek, there seems every need, and naturally Aunt Phoebe feels particularly responsible for you whilst you are in her care."

"Tell Lady Ashley that Bella is an excellent nurse and knowledgeable of many cures. She can care for me better than anyone."

"I will tell her," Emma vowed as she went towards the door, "but I don't expect her to heed me."

When she had gone Annabel drew a sigh. "Do you think Lady Ashley will really call in a physician?"

"Can't rightly say, miss, but it's likely. There'll be an army of leeches growing rich and fat in this town, and Lady Ashley will no doubt have her favourite."

"If she does then I shan't be able to feign illness for much longer."

"Most of those so-called doctors will not be able to tell, you may be sure."

Hardly reassured, Annabel got out of bed once more and walked slowly to the window, gazing down at the busy street-scene below. The ladies and gentlemen strolling by were all fashionably dressed and the

servants in various liveries going about their
business looked imposing too. Carriages,
many with coats of arms emblazoned upon
them, rumbled along the street and as she
watched she suddenly ached to be a part of
it, to live as Georgia Beaumont for the week
or so the pretence would last. Only the
thought of meeting Lord Cranbourne again
as an equal held her back.

She sank down into an armchair and it
was not much later that Emma, as usual in
an excited manner, came bursting into the
room.

"Oh, see what has only just arrived for
you, Georgia!"

She was carrying a basket of flowers.
"For me?" Annabel asked incredulously.
"Who could possibly. . . .?"

"Can you not hazard a guess, Georgia?"

A vague uneasiness began to assail her
and stubbornly she answered, "I know no
one in Bath as yet."

"Oh, you are the most exasperating creature alive! You know very well who has
sent them. Lord Cranbourne. Coyness does
not become you."

Noticing at last that Annabel was in a

chair she put the basket down and the other girl continued to stare at it. "I am so glad you are feeling better, my dear."

Annabel transferred her attention to her at last, her eyes wide with fear. "Oh no! I am not. I feel much, much worse!"

Candles had been lit in all the sconces which mirrored the flickering lights. Bella drew the curtains across the windows and the sounds in the street below grew more indistinct.

"There is a gala evening at the Sydney Hotel," the abigail informed the rather subdued Annabel. "All manner of conveyances are making their way towards it."

"It will be a colourful scene. No doubt we should have been attending too." She looked up at the woman. "Bella, there is no need for you to remain here with me all the time. It isn't as though I am truly ill and in need of nursing."

She came to straighten the counterpane. "Methinks I had better in the event Miss Daunty returns. You're like to strangle her before long, and that would never do."

Annabel laughed. "I am already exceeding fond of the chit, but if she continues with this childish insistance of making a match of me and Cranbourne, I might well be tempted to make an end of her."

"Aye," the maid agreed, "it would never do to encourage that attachment."

Once more Annabel's self-imposed solitude was interrupted; this time a maidservant ushered in an elderly gentleman wearing an old-fashioned tie wig and a none too clean frockcoat.

"Dr. Grisdale to see Miss Beaumont."

He bowed low before her and Annabel stiffened as he said. "Ah, this is the young lady who is the invalid."

"I am no such thing," she protested, "and moreover I did not ask you to call."

"I am here at the specific request of Lady Ashley, who is perturbed, to say the least, by your incapacity."

"Dr. Grisdale, my incapacity cannot be cured by any means at your disposal."

Not to be put off he persisted, "Lady Ashley has acquainted me with the cause of your indisposition, ma'am, and 'tis no wonder your sensibilities are overset."

With no more ado he crossed the room and, seating himself by the bed, proceeded to count her pulse. Looking furious she had no choice but to allow him to do so.

" 'Tis plain you are far from well, ma'am," he pronounced after a moment and Annabel gave Bella a despairing look over his head. "Nevertheless, I have treated such cases often and most successfully. I am persuaded your condition can be considerably improved by my opening a vein and letting a little blood. So, ma'am, if you would kindly co-operate. . . ."

As he began to unpack his instruments Annabel jumped to her feet. "Oh, enough of this tarradiddle! My nerves are perfectly healthy and I will not suffer you to bleed me. Off with you this minute!"

He looked at her in alarm. "Ma'am you are only exciting your nerves to a greater degree by such behaviour. I beg of you submit quietly. It will be much more to your benefit."

"A bleeding cannot benefit me, Dr. Grisdale, of that you may be sure."

"Allow me to know what is best for you, my dear Miss Beaumont. Allow me to continue with no further delay which can only invite ill humours. I have treated many cases such as yours."

"You would not know how to treat a sick cow."

The physician drew back in alarm. "Ma'am, you are in more need of my ministrations than you can know."

"Oh, enough of this," she declared, waving her hand in the air. "If I was ill, be certain that I am now quite recovered, I thank you."

Dr. Grisdale was understandably surprised by so sudden a transformation of his patient but in the face of such determination he quickly repacked his instruments and, before bowing out of the room, left a powder on the table to be taken immediately.

The moment he had gone Annabel swept if off the table with an impatient hand. "The old fraud."

Bella was hard put not to laugh. "A fine pair of them you make, then, miss."

Annabel had to laugh too. "What am I to do now?"

"Well, 'tis plain you cannot feign illness any longer, miss. If you continue to fight off physicians in such a way you're like to end up in Bedlam."

Annabel sighed. "Then I fear I shall have

to step out into Bath society after all, and face what comes, Bella."

"Aye, and from what I have observed so far, miss, you'll make a better deal of it than Miss Georgia herself!"

FIVE

Having been defeated in her first objective
Annabel put on a cheerful face the following morning. Wearing one of Georgia's gowns
of cream sprigged muslin she attended breakfast feeling somewhat abashed and fearing
what Dr. Grisdale might have told Lady
Ashley.

Emma was already eating a hearty breakfast and with her mouth full of bread and
butter declared, "Oh, you do look robust
today. Fortunately you have chosen a health-
ful town in which to be ill. Aunt Phoebe
vouches for the beneficial properties of the
waters."

Annabel sat down and a servant brought her some coffee. Lady Ashley now joined them.

"How nice to see you so hearty again, Georgia."

"Thank you, Lady Ashley, but I fear my complexion owes a great deal to the hare's-foot and rouge."

As she spoke Annabel was once more assailed by guilt, and then she reasoned that if anyone should experience guilt it must be Georgia Beaumont, which cheered her somewhat.

Still wary she watched Lady Ashley as she seated herself at the table. Gowned becomingly in pale blue satin, she displayed no sign of the lethargy of Annabel's arrival and seemed quite robust herself.

"Dr. Grisdale is a marvel," she enthused. "I only wonder that I didn't call him in a day earlier rather than allow you to wallow in illness for so long."

"What . . . what did Dr. Grisdale report to you?" Annabel asked hesitantly.

"That your nerves were completely over-set by your experience, and that he had administered a powder which was bound to be effective. *Voilà,* so it is."

Annabel smiled to herself and settled down to enjoy a wafer-thin slice of ham. What a mountebank, she thought. No doubt he had also earned a massive fee for his services. She was beginning to learn that she was only one of a number of tricksters who attached themselves to the *haute monde,* although her own brand of trickery would not last out the week.

"I have written to your mama," Lady Ashley went on, startling Annabel again, "to inform her of your safe arrival. Needless to say, I refrained from telling her of your unfortunate encounter with that scoundrel. There is no point in alarming her unduly, as you came to no real harm."

"That is very thoughtful of you, Lady Ashley."

"I am glad you agree.

"Ah, I see you are wearing the pearl necklet I had made for you." Annabel's hand went to it automatically but by then Lady Ashley had gone on, "Bath water will complete your recovery, my dear, and we shall make haste to the Pump Room immediately breakfast is over. Not only is it conducive to your health, but everyone of consequence will be there. I am not sure which consideration is the more important. In your case, perhaps the latter."

She smiled with satisfaction whilst Annabel took a deep breath, aware she was on the brink of being launched into Bath society in the guise of Georgia Beaumont, heiress. At the thought she was almost tempted to take to her bed again, but she had a stout heart and silently determined to see the ordeal through for Georgia Beaumont's sake alone.

The Pump Room was so crowded that all the fashionables present found themselves hard pressed to see and be seen. While Lady Ashley went to be dipped in the King's Bath, Emma undertook to introduce Annabel to the ritual of the Pump Room where, beneath crystal chandeliers and a stern countenanced statue of the late Beau Nash, ordinary people rubbed shoulders with nobility and took the waters for the benefit of their health. An orchestra played discreetly but few enough present actually listened to their efforts, and anyway, the music was all but drowned by the noise of talking and laughter.

Annabel found she did not like the taste of the water and merely sipped at her glass whilst Emma looked around her with eyes that shone with speculation and excitement.

"You must take the prescribed two glasses for the waters to be of any benefit," Emma scolded when Annabel discarded her glass at last.

"You would not have me ill again, would you?"

"Fudge, it will do you nothing but good. It has worked wonders for Aunt Phoebe, who was quite ill when she first arrived."

"Well, I have an excellent constitution and you know full well visitors come here for only social reasons."

Emma eyed her wryly. "You really are too outspoken to be fashionable, Georgia. Moreover, you are quite unlike the person Aunt Phoebe led me to expect."

"Lady Ashley has not seen ... me for sixteen years."

"She declares you have changed out of all recognition."

"Two-year-old girls usually do."

Several people came up to them whom Emma was glad to introduce to Annabel and they spent some considerable time conversing. Much to her relief the subject-matter was of a general sort. No one mentioned

Lord Cranbourne or the highwayman, although she felt they wished to, and as Georgia Beaumont had not spent any time in London, Annabel was not expected to know anyone, which was a blessing.

After a while Annabel found she was actually enjoying herself. For once she was not being overlooked as an unimportant servant, or pitied by those who usually did not deem to notice her existence, nor was she forced to be subservient at all times to some peevish invalid. The freedom from those tyrannies almost caused her head to swim and the fact she was being looked upon as a person of import and interest suited her very well she discovered. It was gratifying to have so many people of consequence seek out her company, not to mention the gentlemen who looked upon her with undisguised admiration, and she could not for anything understand Georgia Beaumont's repugnance of the place. So far it seemed quite delightful.

As she chattered unselfconsciously to one of Lady Ashley's friends and her daughter, a girl a of similar age to Annabel herself, she became aware of a ripple of excitement in the room and, on glancing round, had no difficulty in recognising the cause of it. Lord Cranbourne had arrived, and as he stood head and shoulders above everyone else in the room she saw him immediately.

At about the same time Emma Daunty spotted him too and unceremoniously elbowed Annabel, who affected not to notice. All the same, it was difficult for her to continue with general conversation. Momentarily, her eyes met his across the room, but he made no sign that he recognised her and was engaged in conversation. She did not know whether to feel injured or relieved. However, after some time had passed she began to realise he was gradually moving closer until at last she became uncomfortably aware that he was standing next to her.

"Miss Beaumont," he said as if only just becoming aware of her presence, "What a happy incidence this is."

Annabel did not doubt that everyone in the room was aware of the meeting and watching anxiously for any developments, which did nothing to calm her ruffled demeanour.

"Lord Cranbourne, I did not look to see you here," she answered, a mite uncomfortably.

"One does not need to be an invalid, and propriety decrees that a morning visit to the Pump Room is not to be missed."

She was not certain whether there was any irony in his voice, but when she looked at him it was to discover that he was surveying her carefully, which caused her cheeks to grow pink.

"I am relieved to see you so much recovered from your indisposition, Miss Beaumont."

Annabel did not know whether it was *bon ton* or not to thank him for his flowers and calls, and because of that and the fact she had not really been ill at all she became a trifle irritated at the unending concern which had been voiced that morning.

Averting her eyes she answered, "It would be gratifying if the matter was allowed to lapse. Now that I am in perfectly good health I am growing heartily sick of the subject."

She could sense Emma's outrage and she was already regretting being sharp with him, but whatever Lord Cranbourne's reaction to her rudeness may have otherwise been Emma stepped in to say quickly:

"We are all aware, Lord Cranbourne, that Georgia's indisposition would have been far more serious had you not come to her rescue."

"Miss Daunty, you must not exaggerate what was a very small service, as Miss Beaumont will agree, I am sure."

His voice was cold and clipped and Annabel was hard pressed not to shiver. Despite her attempts to put him off she decided she did not like at all his coldness and infinitely preferred to have his good will.

"On the contrary, Lord Cranbourne, it was magnificent of you to do what you did, risking your own well-being for my sake."

She did not know if her words acted as a balm, for she dare not look at him.

"In any event," Emma went on, "Dr. Grisdale soon put her to rights with one of his own potions."

The marquis glanced at her curiously. "So Dr. Grisdale has attended you; you are to be considered more fortunate than anyone imagines for your quick recovery."

Emma laughed heartily, saying, "Lord Cranbourne, you must not allow my aunt to hear you say so. She vouches for his remedies."

Annabel could not help but smile at his assessment of the physician, which so nearly matched her own.

"I can only praise a physician who restores someone to health so skillfully," he added, and then, bowing stiffly, "By your leave, ladies."

They both watched him go and then, when he was out of earshot, Emma rounded on her new-found friend. "Georgia, how could you snub him so?"

"Tush! I did no such thing."

"You knew exactly what you were about. Do you not realise how eligible he is? That most girls would give their ears to be addressed by him, let alone receive flowers?"

Annabel's answer was to turn away from Emma's well-meaning meddling. In truth she did not know why she was so desperate to cut the marquis, except that she was aware of a necessity to avoide close relationships with anyone in Bath. Her tenure on the name of Beaumont was bound to be a short one. Already half the week had passed; Georgia Beaumont may yet be wed and on her way home. A letter could be on its way to her and the thought gave her an unexpected pang of sorrow.

Through one of the Pump Room windows bathers in the King's Bath could be seen, enveloped in canvas gowns and wearing straw hats. Annabel's glance sought out the countess and then when she did catch sight of her she moved away again, telling Emma, "Lady Ashley is being taken from the bath. I think it is time we went to join her."

A subscription ball was being held at Harrison's Assembly Rooms the following evening and Lady Ashley had declared her intention to go. The three ladies had spent a pleasant day, first visiting the Pump Room where, to Annabel's relief, Lord Cranbourne did not appear, and she was able to enjoy light conversations with several new acquaintances. After leaving the Pump Room, Lady Ashley had acquainted Annabel with the delightful shops in Milsom Street, making several extravagant purchases on her supposed goddaughter's behalf. Annabel decided to accept the kidskin gloves and the beaded reticule gratefully, determining that later she would leave them with all the rest of Georgia's belongings once the charade was over.

After a delightful dinner at Pulteney Street, Lady Ashley's town carriage conveyed them the short distance to the Lower Assembly Rooms which were situated on the banks of the Avon where the evening's events were to take place.

All three ladies were gowned beautifully, Annabel in apricot muslin, Emma in yellow sarsenet, and Lady Ashley wearing brown taffeta with a matching feathered turban.

"I forgot to tell you, my dear," the countess said as the carriage set off from Pulteney Street, "I have received a letter from your mama." Annabel looked at her anxiously. "She sends love from all at Hetherington Howard."

Annabel smiled faintly. "I am obliged to you for keeping her informed, Lady Ashley, for I am sadly lax in my correspondence."

"Are not all young ladies? I recall I was too at your age."

"I have not written to my mama for a week," Emma declared. "She will think me sadly remiss."

Lady Ashley was eyeing Annabel consideringly. "There was, I understand, quite a to-do before you left for Bath."

Once again Annabel raised her eyes and Lady Ashley went on to explain, "Did not Edgar fancy himself in love with some creature your mama had employed as a companion?"

Again Annabel smiled faintly. "Oh, yes, indeed." When it appeared she was expected to say more, with great discomfort she added, "It was exceedingly foolish of him, for the young lady gave him no encouragement whatsoever."

"Your mama declares that she did, most emphatically."

"It isn't true!" Annabel cried and then, realising she was growing too heated on the subject, fell silent.

"Ah, well," the countess sighed, "Ada's judgment in such matters was never sound."

"I always pity such creatures who are forced to seek employment in so ingratiating a fashion," Emma declared, much to Annabel's chagrin. "My Aunt Flavia Birkwood, you know—has had a companion for years, and a merry dance she leads her too. I declare if she were a dog she would have bitten her savagely before now."

Lady Ashley laughed and Emma went on, addressing herself to Annabel now, "Really, I cannot conceive what Mr. Beaumont was about, for I'm persuaded that she was as plain as a pipe-stem. These creatures invariably are."

Annabel immediately bridled. "She is quite

handsome. Edgar is not such a chuckle-head as you suppose."

Emma immediately became downcast and Lady Ashley remarked, " 'Tis plain the creature earned Georgia's admiration. Paid companions are in such invidious positions, and your mama, if you will forgive me for saying so, is not the easiest lady to please. There are times when she would find fault with a fat goose."

Immediately Annabel warmed toward Georgia's godmother. She was now convinced that her friendship with Mrs. Beaumont could only have lasted in the face of prolonged separation. They were the most unlikely friends she had ever encountered.

"It has occurred to me that I would enjoy the company of a person such as the one Mrs. Beaumont dismissed. I have seriously been considering employing a companion for an age."

"Aunt Phoebe," Emma cried, "what need have you for such services?"

"Once you girls have departed I believe I shall feel lonely, and recall that I have no son or indeed a husband who might be distracted by her." She smiled at Annabel, "What a pity this particular young lady will be miles away in some unknown place by now. La! I shall have to secure the services of another."

Annabel opened her mouth to speak but, having nothing to say, closed it again. How galling it was not to be able to speak up, for a situation with Lady Ashley, who was so kind, could hardly be bettered.

The carriage was forced to slow down because of the dense traffic on the road to the Assembly Rooms. Lady Ashley embraced both girls with another smile.

"We are almost there. I do hope both you girls will enjoy the evening ahead. 'Tis not London, of course . . ."

She looked at Annabel, who was moved to say, "Compared to Hetherington Howard, Bath is a veritable whirl of activity."

"Indeed it will be divine," Emma enthused, and then, glancing slyly at Annabel, "Naturally, one hopes Georgia will not scandalise everyone by snubbing Lord Cranbourne."

Lady Ashley gave Annabel another considering look before answering her niece's accusation. "There is nothing to say Lord Cranbourne will be present tonight; after all, he is probably in Bath to see his *chère amie,* who lodges in Landsdowne. However, if Georgia does decide not to encourage his advances it is her prerogative to do so."

Emma stared at her aunt in astonishment. Indeed, so did Annabel, for Lady Ashley's attitude was quite odd in view of the reason Georgia was supposed to be in Bath, and far from being glad of her support Annabel left the carriage feeling distinctly uneasy.

SIX

The atmosphere in the Assembly Rooms was a gay one, sufficient to raise Annabel's spirits immediately. Together with activities at the Upper Assembly Rooms, which were situated in Alfred Street, there were sufficient balls to keep the visitors and residents occupied each evening.

Almost immediately on their arrival Lady Ashley retired to the card-room and was soon engaged in a rubber of whist, leaving the girls free to mix as they wished. The Master of Ceremonies ensured the dancing was well organised, and both Emma and Annabel were soon engaged for several sets.

Although Annabel was enjoying herself far more than she had envisaged she would at the outset, she still envied Emma's whole-hearted glee at every diversion offered. Annabel only wished she was free to emulate her.

During the supper interval Lady Ashley rejoined them, ascertaining that all was well with them.

"This is excellent preparation for your London season, Emma," she told her niece.

"I can scarce await that time. If only Georgia could join me for my début."

Lady Ashley gave Annabel a smile. "I fancy Georgia will be wed by then, my dear, but I am certain you will remain friends."

To Annabel's relief the music started up and her next partner came to claim her. Lady Ashley's attitude continued to irk her, but after a short while she put it out of her mind.

It was only after she had stood up for several sets that she became aware that at some point in the evening Lord Cranbourne had arrived. She could not help but notice, as many others had, that he was the most imposing man in the room. His looks, she realised yet again, were more than noteworthy, and many ladies were casting him admiring and flirtatious glances. His coat was of the best superfine, adorned by plain gold buttons and several chains and fobs, and his neckcloth was perfectly folded with a modicum of lace on his shirt.

"You can tell the Brummell influence, can you not?" Emma whispered in her ear, echoing her own thoughts most uncomfortably.

Annoyed at being caught looking at him at all Annabel retorted, "I cannot admire any man who slavishly obeys another. Everyone must develop his own style."

"I do not doubt Cranbourne has a deal of style which sets him apart from others, but he and Brummell are the greatest friends, both a part of Prinny's Carlton House Set. Brummell often gives Lord Cranbourne his arm along St. James's Street, and they are seen in the window of White's together."

Despite her own prejudice Annabel was impressed and said, "If that is so, I cannot conceive what he is about in Bath."

Emma chuckled. "Oh, I can."

Suddenly, looking around him with a languid air, the marquis caught sight of Annabel and began to move towards her.

On noting his intention Emma said, "Mr.

Dollingsby is partnering me in this set so I must go and join him now."

"Oh please don't . . ." Annabel begged, but it was too late.

It was also too late for her to avoid the marquis's attention so she resolved to be cool towards him, yet remain polite.

"Good evening, Miss Beaumont," he said somberly, subjecting her to that searching look which most females seem to find totally devastating.

"Lord Cranbourne," she responded, averting her eyes, for she was considerably discomforted herself.

After a moment's uncomfortable silence he said, "May I bespeak one of the country dances with you?"

"I am afraid I am engaged for most of them." Slowly she raised her eyes which came level with the diamond pin fixed in his neck-cloth. "It seems, Lord Cranbourne, that I have been somewhat churlish with you."

"That is of no account, Miss Beaumont, I assure you. I fear it may be due to my behaviour on a previous encounter."

She looked into his face then and he smiled, "It is evident that you do not recall."

"Do you mean on the road to Bath, Lord Cranbourne?"

"It was many years before that."

Annabel's head reeled at this unexpected blow. "I assure you I have no notion what you mean."

"It is as I thought. Your parents brought you to Maingay Chase for a shooting weekend. You were but a child at the time, so it is not surprising that you don't recall, although I feared that you would."

Her heart was beating fast. Surely it couldn't be that he had encountered Georgia Beaumont at some previous time. Her ears *must* be deceiving her.

"Be assured I am relieved that you do not recall, Miss Beaumont, for I had little time or patience for a young girl, and I feared you might still resent it."

She swallowed noisily. "Lord Cranbourne, I . . . assure you I have no memory of the occasion." She managed to smile at him coyly then, although her mind was still in a whirl. "It is remiss of me, is it not?"

"Not at all. We have both greatly changed. I was hard put to recognise you at all."

Her laughter was loud and she hoped it did not sound quite so false as it was. "From what people tell me the change was not only desirable but necessary in me."

"It certainly is to your advantage, ma'am."

Flustered, she fluttered her fan. "Oh, if only you had told me earlier."

"You might have treated me with greater disdain, and that was my fear."

"You must forgive me my churlishness, for it was not due to any action on your part. The truth is that I did not want to come to Bath, but was forced to do so by circumstances not entirely within my control."

"Young ladies of breeding rarely have control of their own destinies. It is most unfair, especially as I feel that you are not one to bow easily to the wishes of others."

Annabel's fan fortunately hid her pink cheeks as she replied, "I am not certain that you flatter me, my lord."

Out of the corner of her eye she could see that Emma was watching them anxiously in between conversing with a sallow-faced young woman of a similar age to her own.

"Be certain that I do."

She gave him her attention again. "Do you intend to stay in Bath for long?"

"A little while longer in any event," he answered with maddening vagueness.

"You surprise me. Do you not find this town a trifle dull after the diversions of London?"

"On the contrary, ma'am, I am enjoying myself hugely."

"Again you surprise me. From what I am given to understand, you would find Bath devilishly dull."

"Whoever said so is mistaken. There is so much to enjoy here, not the least charming company."

"Aside from the charming company, what is there for a man to enjoy in Bath? I have yet to discover what there is to attract a man of your standing, Lord Cranbourne. I am persuaded you do not need to take the waters."

He smiled slightly and Annabel felt that they were indulging in some kind of a duel of words, in which he was bound to be the winner.

"It is gratifying that you are so interested. Let me assure you the charming company I encounter at every turn is reason enough, but in a few days' time Claverton Down will see a mill between two of the best pugilists in the south of England. If I were not here, I would miss it, would I not?"

"Gentlemen enjoy the oddest diversions, Lord Cranbourne."

He smiled urbanely once again. "So do ladies, from all I have observed."

Emma was coming towards them and Annabel didn't know whether to be relieved or not. The girl curtsied prettily before saying, "Is this not the most delightful gathering, Lord Cranbourne?"

"I entirely agree with you, Miss Daunty. Nothing London has to offer could possibly compare."

He glanced at Annabel, who shot him an angry look, for she was certain he was mocking her now although Emma did not note it. She merely giggled.

"Later, Georgia, when you have a minute or two to spare, Isobel Fairbrough would like words with you."

"Isobel Fairbrough?"

"From what she tells me she is an old friend from the academy you attended. Surely you recall her. She recalls you very well and cannot wait to renew the acquaintance."

Annabel looked around to where the sallow-faced girl was peering myopically across the room at her. The picture of her grew blurred and she swayed slightly on her feet. The entire venture was fast turning into a nightmare. First Lord Cranbourne had met her before and now Georgia's old schoolfriend. Of the two Isobel Fairbrough was much the more dangerous, for she had known Georgia more recently and intimately. She would not be fooled at all.

Suddenly, Annabel recovered her calm and clutched on to the marquis's coat sleeve, much to his amazement.

"I cannot speak with her now, Emma. I am engaged for this set with Lord Cranbourne."

Although he was evidently startled at her change of heart the marquis was gallant enough to lead her on to the dance-floor where sets were being made up for a gavotte.

"Are you not anxious to greet an old schoolfriend?" he inquired as the orchestra struck up once more.

She laughed gaily. "Isobel Fairbrough was never a close friend of mine, and I am in no way anxious to renew the acquaintance."

A slow smile crossed his face. "I understand perfectly. I am often accosted by people I'd as lief not converse with; they can be devilishly boring."

She drew an almost indiscernible sigh at

his interpretation of her fear. As the gavotte progressed she came to realise that he cut a very dashing figure and not once trampled her toes, which was more than could be said of many of her partners that evening.

All too soon the gavotte came to an end and after escorting her to the edge of the dance-floor excused himself. No doubt, Annabel though vexedly as she watched him go, the lure of the gaming-tables drew him inexorably.

There was no time for her to ponder on the enigmatic marquis, for Emma and Isobel Fairbrough were approaching. Annabel succumbed to the urge to flee the room, but before she had reached the door she was accosted by a gentleman with whom she had become acquainted and allowed him to lead her on to the dance-floor. After having danced with the marquis, Annabel found this gentleman rather tiresome, but at least he prevented Isobel Fairbrough approaching yet again.

As Emma was invariably engaged to dance, Annabel found it easy to avoid Georgia's old schoolfriend, and when it seemed the girl had gone at last she drew a sigh of relief although she was realistic enough to know she had not seen the last of that particular girl, and she would not be able to avoid her indefinitely.

"Did you manage to have a coze with Isobel?" Emma asked when they met again as the candles burned low in their sockets.

"Unfortunately not. I have been engaged for most of the evening, and the opportunity did not arise."

Emma's eyes twinkled merrily. "So I have observed; with Lord Cranbourne for a good deal of it too."

"You exaggerate as is usual, Emma," Annabel told her irritably. "I stood up with him but once."

"But how long you conversed before then! I told you you would find his company congenial, did I not?"

"Stuff and nonsense. My feelings have not changed a jot, but after the service he did me I must at least be civil."

"If you are not a great deal more than civil I would think your attic's to let, but I'm persuaded you will agree his company is much more to be desired than that of Isobel Fairbrough."

Annabel gave her a curious look before

saying, in a carefully controlled voice, "I do entirely agree."

"After several moments of conversation I was bound to conclude she is a dowd and a tiresome bore."

Eagerly now Annabel went on, "Why do you think I have been trying to avoid her? She was always the most tiresome creature at the academy, and so difficult to put off, as you have no doubt discovered. Emma," she went on eagerly, "will you be my ally?"

"Naturally," the girl agreed. "What would you have me do?"

"Simply keep her away from me whenever you can. I have no inclination to renew the acquaintance. Moreover, she is a prattlebox of the most imaginative kind."

"It will be my pleasure to help you, even if it does mean that I am burdened with her company instead."

Annabel gave her a grateful smile and hoped the girl would not recognise a look of relief when she saw one.

"Oh, I say . . ." Emma gasped, gazing across the room.

The surprise in her voice caused Annabel to look up too, and she immediately stiffened on seeing a very handsome woman, exquisitely dressed in a white satin gown liberally appliqued with seed pearls, on the arm of none other than the Marquis of Cranbourne.

The picture they presented was one of complete harmony and, as such a good-looking pair, attracted no small amount of interest. If no other man in the room equalled the marquis, then most certainly his companion could rival the handsomest of the ladies present.

The woman was, in truth, little older than Annabel herself, but she had an air about her which indicated greater maturity, making Annabel feel not only childish, but a dowd too.

"Mrs. Foxwood," Emma whispered in answer to Annabel's unspoken question. "Is she not divine?"

"She is exceeding handsome," Annabel admitted, albeit reluctantly. "*Who* is she?"

"His *chère amie*. It was a well-known liaison until some time ago when it was rumoured she had fallen out of favour. For a while she was seen in the company of a Colonel Lefevre, but he is at present fighting the Frenchies, so obviously this is why Lord Cranbourne is back in Bath. Such passions do not easily die. Only see the diamonds at her throat and wrist. It is much more than any wife might expect."

"From all I have observed Cyprians are better treated than mere wives, Emma. I am only surprised he has the impudence to bring her here."

"Oh, in Bath no one really cares, Georgia."

Annabel caught his eye at that moment and then she deliberately turned away. "If I had known his doxy was present I would not have stood up with him."

Emma looked at her in amazement. "Georgia, I had no notion you were so unsophisticated. You have the opportunity of inviting an offer of marriage; you must not allow such sensibilities to prevent a brilliant match. I should not. It is our duty to our families to marry well."

It was Annabel's turn to look amazed. "Emma, there is no possible chance . . ."

"He is ripe for marriage and dangling for an heiress too. I'm persuaded you could not suit him better."

"I thought he was the owner of considerable wealth of his own." Annabel replied, giving her a curious look.

"Cranbourne and his cronies live expensively. Naturally, they have massive incomes, but it does not always suffice. Like Prinny himself they are always in dun territory."

"So they are obliged to seek out a Smithfield Bargain," she murmured echoing Georgia Beaumont's own words.

The other girl laughed heartily at that, before answering, "It can be a happy arrangement, you know. One is not obliged to take a husband in dislike merely because he is chronically out of funds."

Before she could say any more, and there was a great deal she could say on the subject. Annabel had caught sight of Lady Ashley.

"I believe your aunt is beckoning to us. It must be time to leave," Annabel said in some relief and, as they left the room, she could not prevent herself glancing back to see Mrs. Foxwood still clinging to Lord Cranbourne's arm and he in conversation with her. Despite the fact he meant absolutely nothing to her, she could not help the quiver of anger she felt towards him, nor her envy of the lovely Mrs. Foxwood.

SEVEN

Sleep did not come easily to Annabel that night despite her exhaustion after the day's events. She was uneasily aware that she could not for ever avoid a confrontation with Isobel Fairbrough, even with Emma's help, or indeed anyone else acquainted with Georgia Beaumont. For all Annabel knew, Bath might be full of people acquainted with the girl, for in such a short space of time she had encountered two people who had met her previously. Annabel's only cheering thought was that she should have news from the eloping couple any day now, but even that notion cast her into the dismals, for she was truly enjoying life in Bath. That included, she now admitted to herself, her encounters with the marquis, and it was with thoughts of him that she finally fell asleep to dream they were dancing a cotillion together in some enchanted garden.

She went down to breakfast the following morning, looking somewhat hollow-eyed, and found herself being regarded critically by Lady Ashley.

"You seemed to have enjoyed yourself last night," she murmured.

"It was . . . tolerably pleasant," Annabel answered. "Did you?"

The countess laughed. "Fortune was not with me, I fear, but it was pleasant enough, I own. Sir Darley Pont still believes I will accept his offer of marriage, but in truth I only wish to win his guineas!"

"If I may take the liberty of saying so," Annabel ventured, "you are far too young to remain a widow."

The countess picked up her cup and looked thoughtful. "Oh, his is not the only offer I have received since Ashley died. In fact, I have lost count of them, but in my opinion, my dear, a woman should remain a widow rather than marry a man she cannot love wholeheartedly. Besides," she added, "I am perfectly happy with no man to say I should not gamble when I enjoy gaming so thoroughly."

"Do you ever game with Lord Cranbourne?" Annabel could not help asking.

At this Lady Ashley laughed heartily. "I may play deep, my dear, but not *that* deep."

She was thoughtful for a moment and then, recalling her anxiety to hear from Georgia, asked, "Have any communications arrived for me?"

"No, my dear. Were you expecting one?"

"Not . . . particularly."

Lady Ashley smiled and then continued with her breakfast. "Not even from some secret lover?"

"No!"

The older woman laughed at her outrage. "There is no need for you to look so abashed, my dear. All young ladies have secret lovers."

"Georgia does not," Emma answered as she came into the room. "There is nothing secret about Lord Cranbourne's intentions."

Annabel shot her an angry look before answering, "I care nothing for his intentions. The man's attic is to let if he believes he can

pay court to me in the same room as he
entertains his light-skirt."

The countess laughed, much to Annabel's
surprise. "My dear, if you harbour such
sensitive feelings, I fear you will never wed,
for there are few enough men worth the
name who do not support another household." Giving Annabel a hard look she went
on, "However, I rather think the cause of
your considerable spleen may be an excess
of wine rather than a disgust of Mrs.
Foxwood. This morning, Georgia, you shall
come with me to the King's Bath to be
dipped."

"Oh no, Lady Ashley . . ."

"*Yes,* Georgia, I insist upon it. It is certain
to soothe your nerves and restore your constitution. I am very tempted to call in Dr.
Grisdale after the benefits of his last visit."

Annabel lapsed into silence once more
and decided philosophically that she might
as well agree with everything, for as long as
the situation lasted. Anything was better
than a visit from the fraudulent Dr. Grisdale.

Dutifully, Annabel allowed herself to be
undressed and enveloped in a canvas gown
which hid all her womanly charms, and was

dipped in the bath by a burly woman employed to do so.

The water was surprisingly hot and after remaining in the bath for some considerable time she was wrapped in a large towel and conveyed to Pulteney Street to recover.

As she lay on the bed, wondering what benefit anyone could possibly derive from the dip, Bella ventured, "Is there no news from Miss Georgia, ma'am?"

"I am afraid not, Bella. I cannot conceive what the delay can be."

The abigail wrung her hands. "I trust nothing has gone wrong in her plans."

Annabel set up at last certain that a dipping in the Bath waters was far from beneficial, for she experienced only weakness since returning from it.

"I cannot hold how that may be, although it is possible that Miss Beaumont misjudged the time it would take to journey to Gretna and back. Even without consideration for us, Bella, I know Miss Beaumont will wish to inform her family of the news immediately she is wed."

Bella drew a sigh. "Aye, you're right, miss. I've known her since she was a baby and cared for her most of those years. I should not have allowed this to happen."

"Neither should I, Bella, although I'm persuaded if we had not co-operated with her she would have devised an alternative scheme. I fear discovery of our duplicity with every day that passes, and that would bode ill for us all. However," she went on, drawing a sigh, "we have no choice but to continue."

"You look better already," Lady Ashley declared when Annabel emerged from her room at last. She pulled on her gloves and then cast a smile towards Annabel. "A little shopping before dinner is in order. A visit to Milsom Street will soon put the sparkle back in your eyes."

"Lady Ashley," Annabel protested with a laugh. "I am perfectly all right."

She led the way to the waiting carriage. "In health perhaps, but I am not foolish enough to ignore the sadness in your eyes."

Annabel averted her face immediately, stricken with both alarm and remorse. As Lady Ashley settled back in the squabs she added:

"My dear, if you ever wish to have a coze

with me recall I am not your mama but I do have your best interests at heart."

Annabel lowered her head even farther to hide the tears which were pricking at her eyes and did not look up again until the countess said, "Oh, here comes Emma now. Hurry, dear, we are late already."

Emma Daunty came hurrying out of the house, holding on to her bonnet and crying breathlessly, "Oh, I could not find my white kid gloves. They were in the most unlikely place."

As Emma climbed into the carriage and sank back into the squabs next to Annabel, Lady Ashley gave the driver the order to go. As the carriage jerked into movement, Annabel was glad of Emma's inconsequential chatter, although the countess continued to gaze at her consideringly.

The circulating library in Milsom Street was crowded with fashionables, not merely selecting books but meeting socially too. It was an excellent library, a treasure trove to Annabel, who had felt the loss of good reading material while at Hetherington Howard, where books were considered an unnecessary extravagance. Now she was glad of the opportunity of choosing reading material which she hoped might divert her mind from unwelcome thoughts at quiet moments.

Lady Ashley glanced at them before saying, "Such weighty tomes, Georgia. You never cease to surprise me. I had thought Mrs. Radcliffe your limit. Your mama always declared you had nothing but windmills in your head."

She drifted away to greet an acquaintance and just as Annabel was about to draw a sigh of relief she caught sight of Isobel Fairbrough, who was coming purposefully towards her. Fortunately, Emma Daunty saw her too and, true to her word, stepped forward and engaged her in conversation. The girl looked slightly vexed but was too well bred to snub Emma, and Annabel took the opportunity of escaping to another part of the establishment.

As she backed away she bumped into several people including, much to her alarm, Lord Cranbourne.

· "Oh, I do beg your pardon," she gasped before she realised it was he.

He raised his curly-brimmed beaver. "Miss Beaumont. This is indeed a day full of good fortune for me. I have been privileged to see you on two occasions."

"Indeed. I am not aware of a previous one, Lord Cranbourne."

"That does not surprise me. This morning you were brave enough to be dipped in the King's Bath. I trust the experience has benefited your health."

"There is nothing wrong with my health. I visited the bath merely at the bidding of Lady Ashley, who deemed it would be beneficial."

One eyebrow went up a fraction. "I had no notion you were so biddable, Miss Beaumont."

His use of Georgia's name irked her, somewhat illogically, together with the memory of his blatant display of his inamorata.

"That is not so surprising, my lord; you can have no notion of anything concerning me."

She raised her eyes to meet his challengingly. They were a deep, soft brown, not at all cynical.

"If, alas, that is true, perhaps you will allow me to rectify the omission in the coming weeks."

She looked at him again, uncertain whether he was being ironic or not. His manner certainly made her feel uneasy, but there was no way of telling if he were being sincere or not. Her heart grew heavy, for she suspected it was indeed true he needed to marry an heiress, and Georgia Beaumont was as opportune a bargain as any.

His eyes held hers almost hypnotically and despite the crush around them Annabel was suddenly only aware of his presence. Her heart began to beat loudly and she realised that in some way she was tottering on the brink of behaviour even more ruinous than anything which had gone before.

Just as she drew her gaze from his at last and averted her eyes in dismay at the strength of her own feelings, Lady Ashley came bustling up to them, causing the marquis to transfer his attention to the older woman in his usual gallant manner.

"So this is where you are hiding," she greeted them, looking, Annabel noted, more than a little smug.

"Lady Ashley," the marquis said, bowing low, "it is plain to see that the waters of Bath agree with you exceedingly well."

"I thank you, Lord Cranbourne, for that

observation, but I recall that your father was always a most skilful flatterer."

"And I am a practised speaker of the truth."

The countess eyed him speculatively for a moment or two. "I trust that you are," she answered in a soft tone, and then, looking at Annabel once more, she smiled. "I regret having to interrupt this tête-à-tête between you two, but we must leave now. I am expecting guests this evening, one of whom is rather special, so if you will excuse us, Lord Cranbourne I shall have to deprive you of my goddaughter's company."

"I am devastated," he murmured before bowing low.

Annabel cast him a final glance before following Lady Ashley towards the entrance. "Am I acquainted with your special guest?" she asked, her mind only barely on what she was saying, for Emma was still holding Isobel Fairbrough in conversation, and the girl looked vexed at being denied access to Annabel once again.

"I believe so," the countess replied with maddening vagueness, and then, waving imperiously to her niece, swept out into the street. Emma joined them at the roadside moments later where the carriage awaited them.

"What did Miss Fairbrough have to say today?" Annabel asked anxiously.

"Nothing of any import," the girl replied. "Naturally, she indicated her anxiety at not being able to speak to you as yet, and then she chattered on about inconsequential matters which almost had me yawning in public."

The news caused Annabel to draw a small sigh of relief but as she got into the carriage Lady Ashley said, "Really, Georgia, you *should* have words with that poor girl."

"I am beginning to think," Emma said in her usual breathless manner, "that you only wish me to keep Miss Fairbrough at bay so you may consort with Lord Cranbourne."

"Stuff and nonsense," Annabel retorted as she climbed into the carriage.

"It would not be so unnatural," Lady Ashley told her in a gentle tone. "It is beginning to look as if he is in earnest, so you must think of what you wish to do should he come up to scratch."

Darkly Annabel answered, clenching her hands together inside her muff, "Lady Ashley, I do not wish to think of it."

* * *

In her room later Annabel complained to the only person she could—Bella.

"Oh, if only I could be done with this farce. Daily I encounter Isobel Fairbrough and I fear she cannot be put off for much longer. Worse, Lord Cranbourne is paying court to me—at least I think he is. One can never really tell with these bucks of the *ton*. He might only be amusing himself at my expense, but if he is in earnest this masquerade must end soon."

"It will, miss, never you fear. We must hear from Miss Georgia—or Mrs. Quinton as she will be—any day now."

Annabel wrung her hands together in anguish. "Yes, I am persuaded that is so."

Bella busied herself putting out Annabel's clothes for the evening. Annabel always left the choosing of what she should wear absolutely to the abigail as she acknowledged she was the better equipped to know what was suitable for various occasions.

"It might be that he is in love with you, miss. *You*, not Miss Georgia, I mean. You have not given him credit for that sentiment."

Annabel gave her a startled look. "You cannot be serious in suggesting that."

"It is not unknown, miss."

Once again she had to look away in dismay. "I am persuaded, with gentlemen of Lord Cranbourne's type, a woman's portion is all which attracts them. He will not take kindly to being fooled by a penniless companion."

"Nor will Lady Ashley, but it is too late to consider it now."

As she was being dressed by Bella, Annabel's heart felt heavy. It seemed the masquerade was becoming unbearable with complications neither she nor Georgia Beaumont could have foreseen.

For once she came down the stairs reluctantly, not at all looking forward to the evening at the theatre, despite it being a play she had dearly wished to see. Isobel Fairbrough was certain to be there and so was Lord Cranbourne, the two people who caused her endless alarm.

There might be little opportunity for social intercourse, but the very fact he would be there cast her spirits down, and yet at the same time it excited her too. In her lonely old age she could recall being pursuaded by one of the foremost Corinthians, even if he did believe her to be quite another person.

Talking and laughter could be heard in the drawing-room as she came down the stairs, Georgia Beaumont's jewellery about her person. As she approached the room she determined to continue as before, during what must be her last few days in Bath. She would not lose her nerve now.

Having so decided she went boldly into the drawing-room. Lady Ashley who, as usual, was impeccably gowned and wearing the famed Ashley rubies, turned to greet her immediately.

"Georgia dear, do come in and join us. We are almost ready to go in to dinner. Come along in; I have a surprise for you. Just look who has come to stay!"

As Lady Ashley was speaking a figure detached itself from the group of gentlemen standing to one side of the room. Annabel stared at him, shocked to the very core of her being. The room began to sway slightly; Lady Ashley's smiling face grew blurred. The pretence was over and she was about to be exposed for what she really was, and in the most ignominious way.

Edgar Beaumont looked similarly shocked. His smile of greeting for his sister faltered to be replaced by a look of shock. His jaw dropped and his mouth opened as if he were about to say something.

"La! What a surprise for you," Lady Ashley was saying. "But is it not a delightful one?"

The sound of her voice suddenly had the effect of mobilising Annabel. Before Edgar Beaumont could speak and denounce her she rushed across the room, flinging herself into his arms.

"Oh, Edgar dearest!" she cried, much to the delight of the many matrons in the room. "How wonderful it is to see you here." She stood on tiptoe to kiss his cheek and at the same time whispered, "Do not betray me, Mr. Beaumont, I beg of you. I will explain all to you when we can be alone together." And then for all to hear, "How shabby of you not to let me know you were coming."

Almost fearfully she drew away and he said in a shaky voice, adjusting his neckcloth, "Georgia my dear, it is good to see you in such good heart."

She drew an almost imperceptible sigh of relief and cast him a grateful look.

"Lady Ashley, why did you not tell me Edgar was coming?"

The woman looked coy. "Do you not find the pleasure of his company greater because of the surprise?"

Annabel could not help but smile. "Once I have recovered from the shock, no doubt I shall."

Before any more words could be bandied the butler announced dinner. Aware of Edgar's perplexed glances in her direction, Annabel clung to his arm into the dining-room.

"Where is Georgia?" he hissed as they were about to be seated at the dinner-table.

"Safe and well, I assure you," she replied.

Fortunately she was allowed a small respite when he was seated at the far end of the table next to Emma Daunty, who kept him engaged in conversation throughout dinner despite the straying of his attention in Annabel's direction from time to time. In response to his frequent puzzled looks she cast him faint smiles. Annabel herself was seated between an elderly matron and a rather deaf roué, who was still painted and bewigged in the fashion of an earlier generation. She conversed with them each in turn but with considerable difficulty as she was anxiously waiting for the time when she could speak with Georgia's brother.

The opportunity came unexpectedly when they were about to depart for the theatre, and Edgar, displaying a rare quickness of mind, suggested that Annabel accompany him in his carriage.

"There is room enough for three," Emma declared, much to the couple's vexation, for it was already evident the girl had taken a liking to the young man.

Fortunately, Lady Ashley came to their rescue. "Not this time, dear. I have matters to discuss with you, and no doubt Georgia and her brother have family messages to exchange."

It was Emma's turn to look vexed but she could not gainsay her aunt and Annabel allowed herself to be handed into the carriage by Edgar Beaumont.

Once they were on their way he said, "I believe I am owed an explanation."

Annabel dug her hands into her muff. "Indeed you are, Mr. Beaumont, but first of all I must thank you for not betraying me as you had every right to do."

"I could not do that in all conscience after such a heart-felt plea, and it was a pleasant surprise to discover *you* here when I was expecting to see only my sister. Besides, I have the notion that Georgia is up to some mischief and that you are here at her connivance."

Realising there was nothing left to do save tell the truth and trust to his assistance she bit her lip and said, "Miss Beaumont did not wish to come to Bath, as you may already know . . ."

"Did not the entire household?" he asked in an exasperated tone. "It was a great relief to us all when she departed and we could enjoy some peace, although I am bound to say I was broken-hearted over the person who went with her, so I scarcely noticed her absence." Annabel's cheeks grew rather pink and he ventured a moment later, "If you are here in her stead where is m'sister?"

After hesitating only a second Annabel blurted out, "She has eloped!"

"Eloped!" he cried and then, lowering his voice, "By jove, who is the scoundrel? Only tell me and . . ."

"Mr. Quinton. And I cannot agree he is a scoundrel, Mr. Beaumont. They are truly in love and if I did not believe it was so I would not have been persuaded to take part in this ruse."

"Oh no? Let me tell you, Georgia can be damned persuasive when she chooses, so I hold you in no way responsible for her actions.

"Eloped, has she? I've a mind to set off in pursuit."

Annabel's hand reached out to grip his. "Oh, I beg of you do not even consider it, Mr. Beaumont! You must not. Oh, if I'd known I would never have been prevailed upon to tell you."

To her surprise he smiled. "I cannot fly in the face of such distress, ma'am."

She relaxed then and realising her hand was still upon his she withdrew in embarrassment to the corner of the carriage.

"No doubt you are awaiting news of her marriage."

"I hope to hear any day now. I am becoming most anxious for word."

"With good cause, for all the approbation is like to fall on your head."

"That really is of no account, for I cannot be in more trouble than I am already."

He averted his eyes. "I am fully aware that the blame for that lies squarely on my shoulders. I had no notion you would be treated in such a cavalier fashion."

Her lips curled into the travesty of a smile. "Oh no, Mr. Beaumont? Did you truly think your family would welcome your choice of wife?"

Once again he looked away in embarrassment. "Believe me when I say I was truly sorry that Mama dismissed you so unfairly."

"It is of no account now, Mr. Beaumont," she answered with a sigh. "In any event I could not have remained much longer in your mother's employ. I am most anxious, though, to have your assurance, now you are acquainted with the facts, that you will not betray me."

Unexpectedly he threw back his head and laughed. "Naturally, I will not. It is no account to me whom my tiresome sister weds. Good luck to Mr. Quinton, I say. Moreover, at the present I harbour no kind thoughts towards my interfering and unjust mama. I am only surprised that you, with your great sense of propriety, allowed yourself to be inveigled into this madness. You were very proper in your dealings with me, I recall."

She smiled faintly. "They are very much in love, Mr. Beaumont; we were not. No," she insisted as he began to protest, "you may have harboured some faint infatuation for me because I was the only female available to you at the time, but neither of us could be said to be in love. Moreover, you are heir to a great inheritance and needs must take a wife more suited to your station.

"Now, tell me how you happen to be in Bath. I heard no talk of it while I was in Hetherington Howard, and Miss Beaumont certainly knew nothing of it."

It was his turn to smile. "That is not so surprising as the visit was not planned. You might have realised I would not take kindly to your dismissal, and Mama in her infinite wisdom decided I would benefit from a stay in Bath in order to get over my infatuation for you."

Her eyes opened wide as he began to laugh at the irony of the situation, and moments later when they arrived at the theatre Annabel was laughing too, their eyes streaming with tears.

The Goldsmith play they were about to see could not be half so amusing.

EIGHT

It was, Annabel discovered, enjoyable having Edgar Beaumont in Bath, especially as he was now an ally. Everywhere she went he was close by her side so there could be no doubt in anyone's mind that she was indeed Georgia Beaumont. It made all the difference to her confidence, and she threw herself into the role of Georgia Beaumont with more expertise than she dreamed she possessed.

The fact that no word had yet arrived from the eloping couple did not seem to trouble Edgar in the least although he did admit, as he strolled out of the Pump Room with Annabel one morning:

"I would give a good deal to be present when Mama receives the news."

Annabel was hard pressed to hide a smile. "Shame on you. That is a very wicked sentiment," and then she added, "I would give a good deal to have news of it myself."

"Oh, Georgia is notoriously heedless of others, Miss Haygarth. She will have blissfully forgotten your existence by now."

Annabel looked both hurt and surprised. "She cannot have forgotten Bella, her own personal maidservant, nor her jewels, which I have been wearing. I am persuaded too, Mr. Beaumont, that your sister will not wish to wear my clothes for any longer than absolutely necessary."

The young man was thoughtful for a moment. "What you say, as always, makes sense, but I, for one, shall neither fret nor complain whilst I may avail myself of your company, which is delightful."

"You must strive to overcome this foolish passion for me, Mr. Beaumont," she urged in a whisper.

He grinned. "I am doing so, dear lady, am I not? Why else would I be in Bath? Meanwhile, your company helps to heal the wound."

"Mr. Beaumont," she replied in amused desperation. "You are gammoning me now."

They had come out of the Pump Room into the sunshine which bathed the Abbey Churchyard. Sedan chairmen were rushing to and fro conveying people to and from the baths beneath the shelter of the Colonnade.

Edgar Beaumont glanced at his gold hunter before replacing it in his pocket. "Regretfully, I must leave you for a while. There is an important mill on Claverton Down today, and I am anxious not to miss it."

"Ah, yes, the mill. Lord Cranbourne did mention it to me."

He gave her a considering look. "He has sponsored the Black Man who fights against Battling Benbow. It will be an excellent show."

Out of the corner of her eye Annabel caught sight of Isobel Fairbrough, who was coming into the Abbey Churchyard with a group of people. She groaned and Edgar looked at her curiously.

"Is something amiss, my dear?"

"Oh, indeed there is. The girl who is approaching," she explained hurriedly, "attended an academy with your sister. She has been anxious to address me, no doubt to ascertain I am an imposter, and I have been obliged to avoid her for days."

He chuckled much to her vexation. "I'll wager my sister would not have foreseen that eventuality."

He continued to look amused rather than concerned and she began to back away. "I'm afraid I must hurry away now if I am to avoid her yet again."

As she moved back towards the crowded Pump Room he caught her arm. "Stay where you are, Miss Haygarth. You cannot hope to avoid her for ever."

"I must try."

"It is best that you should face her."

Annabel gave him a look of panic and alarm, for it was now too late to avoid a meeting. The girl walked up to them with a purposeful step. "Miss Beaumont?" she asked, frowning slightly.

"Yes," Annabel answered uncertainly, glancing sideways at Edgar, who had removed his hat and was looking at the girl with polite interest.

"Georgia Beaumont of *Hetherington Howard* in *Hampshire*?"

"Yes."

"Who is this lady?" Edgar asked in a mild tone, affecting a fashionably languid air.

Embarrassed, Annabel answered, "Allow me to introduce Miss Fairbrough. Miss Fairbrough, this is my brother, Edgar Beaumont."

The girl was evidently taken aback. "Mr. Beaumont, I am indeed glad to make your acquaintance. Your sister often spoke of you, but," she looked at Annabel again, "there is a matter which troubles me greatly and has done so since my arrival in Bath; this is *not* the Georgia Beaumont with whom I attended Miss French's Academy."

Annabel felt faint, for there were a number of people eagerly listening to the conversation. However, she was saved the trouble of finding a reply, for Edgar stepped forward, affecting outrage.

"Miss Fairbrough, are you trying to suggest that this is not my sister, or, indeed, the Countess of Ashley's goddaughter?"

Taken aback by his tone she answered, "I am not certain I know what I suggest, sir, but I do know this is not the girl I was acquainted with at school. I cannot conceive that she has changed so drastically I would not recognise her."

"Moreover, she does not recognise you, but I am Edgar Beaumont and this is my sister, and you must agree I should know."

"Yes, but . . ."

"Unless, of course," the young man went on mercilessly, "your eyesight is failing."

He had evidently hit upon a tender nerve, for the girl drew back, growing pale. "Really, sir, I hardly . . ."

"Oh, enough of this," he cried. "How dare you insult my sister, and in public too. She is quite overset by your foolish prattle."

"I do beg your pardon, but . . ."

"In truth, ma'am, I believe you to be a humbug, wishing to enter society by claiming acquaintance with my sister, who plainly does not know you."

"How dare you!" the girl cried. "You are insulting, sir, and I shall not remain here a moment longer. I am persuaded you are not the Beaumonts of my acquaintance, for they were gentlefolk and 'tis evident you are not!"

Turning on her heel she flounced into the Pump Room, watched by an amazed Annabel.

Edgar replaced his curly-brimmed beaver on his pomaded curls, saying with satisfaction, "That, I fancy, sees the end of that little vexation."

Annabel's astonishment soon turned to amusement, but even so she cast him an accusing look. "Oh, Mr. Beaumont, that was very shabby of you."

He grinned engagingly. "Would you have had her denounce you—in public to boot."

"Naturally not, but you were so harsh, and unjustly so too."

He lifted his shoulders slightly. "But the problem is now solved, I fancy. Oh, I know your sensibilities are injured and quite rightly too. Be certain that when this is over I shall call on the chit and apologise personally for my churlishness. When she hears the explanation I am persuaded her romantic heart will quite carry her away."

"She does not look in the least romantically inclined, Mr. Beaumont," Annabel was bound to point out.

He grinned again. "My charm will quite change her mind. However, I don't believe we should tease our minds about so dowdy a creature who is of no importance at all."

"In social terms she is far more important than I am," she pointed out.

"Then shall I seek her out now and explain the truth?"

"No!" she cried laughingly.

"Now that is settled satisfactorily I must be off. Tell Lady Ashley I shall join her later." She nodded and just as he was about to leave her he paused, "My Mama has windmills in her head if she truly believes you would not make a suitable wife for me. I would be the luckiest man alive if you would accept me."

"Mr. Beaumont, I am exceeding fond of you . . ."

He smiled sadly. "I know, Annabel. I know, but my heart remains shattered all the same."

Concerned, she answered, "I would not wish that for anything. You must set your sights on someone of higher birth and fortune, someone like Miss Daunty, who is already in love with you.

He flushed right up to his ears, looking away in confusion. "She is a fetching chit, I'll not deny, but it will be a long time before I can look upon any other woman with the least fondness." He raised his hat in salute to her. "We will meet again later."

As he strode into Cheap Street, Annabel

drew a small sigh. If he persisted in nursing a broken heart, there was precious little she could do to stop him; she was more concerned that he had stopped any mischief issuing from Isobel Fairbrough.

She glanced back at the crowded Pump Room and after a few moments' hesitation reluctantly went back inside. A buzz of conversation met her, all but drowning out the sound of the orchestra, which played on regardless. Over the countless heads she caught sight of Emma, who was obviously seeking her out. As she made her way to join the girl she saw Isobel Fairbrough. Georgia's old schoolfriend paused in the midst of her conversation to cast Annabel an icy look before turning away again quite deliberately.

Whatever the ethics of Edgar's methods, it seemed he had succeeded in staving off that particular danger, but despite that Annabel could feel only heartsick that the end of the pretence was still not in sight.

On arriving at the field designated for the pugilistic confrontation, Edgar Beaumont discovered to his annoyance that many were there before him. Curricles, phaetons, gigs and other carriages of all descriptions, some spanking new and others rather decrepit, were already in place, and as he rode around, the young man discovered with mounting frustration that he was not going to have a good view of the proceedings.

Finally he abandoned his gig and walked around the field in the hope that some acquaintance would issue an invitation to join him. At the same time as he caught sight of Lord Cranbourne, the marquis saw him and waved him over.

Climbing out of his open carriage, the marquis said, "Mr. Beaumont? It *is* Mr. Edgar Beaumont, is it not?"

The young man flushed. "My lord, I am indeed honoured that you remember me."

The marquis smiled. "I recall you were a promising shot, even though a mere boy at the time."

His colour grew even deeper. "I was in such good company I am only surprised I was noticed at all."

"Come and see my bruiser and tell me what you think of him. Your opinion will be welcome."

Edgar was all but overcome by the attention he was receiving and made haste to the marquis's carriage where an enormous Negro was seated. "Feel his muscles, Beaumont. Do you not think he will beat Chalfont's man?"

Edgar obligingly squeezed the pugilist's arm muscles, which were as hard as rock. "There is no doubt of it, Lord Cranbourne. My money will be on this fellow, no doubt about it."

"I am glad to hear you say so. Found him in Jamaica a year or two ago. I'd pit him against anyone's bruiser, Beaumont. Needless to say he keeps me fighting fit too."

"So I observe. I envy you, Lord Cranbourne."

"You have no need to harbour any such feelings. My friend here will gladly do a few rounds with you whenever you wish."

"Really?" Edgar asked in amazement.

"Consider him to be at your disposal while you remain in Bath. I do trust," he added in a considering tone, "you are remaining in the town for some time."

"Oh, yes indeed, as long as my . . . as Miss Beaumont is here."

"Good! Call round at North Parade in the morning and you and I will trade punches with the fellow."

"I am overwhelmed, Lord Cranbourne," Edgar replied, and sounded it too.

The marquis eyed him for a moment or two before saying, "I presume the reason for this visit is to join your sister."

Once again Edgar's cheeks grew pink. "My sis . . . yes, yes," he laughed, "wonderful girl, my sister. Are you . . . er . . . acquainted with her?" he asked as an afterthought.

"We have met," the other man replied dryly and then, "You must join me in my carriage for the mill. We'll have the best vantage-point from here."

The invitation had the effect of casting his worried thoughts of Annabel from his mind. "Indeed. I should be most obliged for I'd resigned myself to seeing only the tops of their heads."

"Then you shall be my guest." He put his hand on Edgar's shoulder. "You must tell me all about your family, Mr. Beaumont. It is many years since I have seen them, but I recall every member was quite, quite charming . . ."

"What a magnificent mill," Edgar enthused when he called in at Pulteney Street the following morning. "Cranbourne's man gave Benbow the licking of his life. I have never enjoyed a mill more."

"Then Lord Cranbourne's man won?" Annabel asked, interested despite herself.

Lady Ashley glanced at her over her embroidery and smiled faintly.

"No doubt of it at all. The Negro is the best pugilist I have ever seen. The black man soon drew Benbow's cork. Cranbourne must have restored his fortunes on that fight." He leaned towards Annabel and asked in a confidential tone. "What is this Miss Daunty has been telling me that Cranbourne is paying court to you?"

Stiffly Annabel answered, "Emma is a tattle-box. She should have held her tongue."

"*She* has no need to," he told her in low tones and then insisted, "Is it true?"

"Indeed it is," Lady Ashley answered for her as she concentrated on the intricate stitches of her embroidery. "And if what we hope ensues your mama will be delighted, Edgar. It is just what she was hoping for."

At this both Annabel and Edgar simultaneously burst out laughing, joined by Lady Ashley, although for quite a different reason.

"It is so fortunate you decided to come,

Edgar. Before you arrived, Georgia was constantly cast into the dismals, but you have succeeded in cheering her where both Emma and I failed." She quickly gathered up her embroidery silks, putting them into their bag. "If you will both excuse me for a while I needs must speak with Cook and arrange the week's menus. La! Almost half your stay over already, Georgia. How time does go."

Annabel was rather subdued when Lady Ashley left the room. Edgar got to his feet and walked to the window, gazing out at the small garden.

"Is it really true about Cranbourne?"

She twisted her hands together. "I have done my utmost to cry off, but it is sometimes difficult without being actually rude to him. Naturally, he believes me to be Georgia Beaumont, which makes all the difference. He is paying court to an heiress," she added, unable to hide her bitterness.

"He obviously does not recall Georgia's previous meeting with him."

"He does. He declares I am much changed, and for the better."

Knowing that in normal circumstances such irony was likely to amuse her he gave her a hard look. "Are you . . . in love with him?"

She gave him a sharp look. "Credit me with more sense than to be taken in by a rake whose words drip honey to the unsuspecting. It would be exceeding foolish of me if I were to fall in love with him, and I'm persuaded you must own I am not *that*."

He stroked his chin thoughtfully. "You protest very eloquently, my dear, but I can think of few females, even eminently sensible ones, who would not throw their caps over the windmill because of a kind word from him."

She didn't attempt to argue with him, but she did give him an anguished look. "What can have become of your sister?"

He sighed. "I do not know and in truth I do not really care. My sister is a selfish chit, putting you in such an invidious position."

"I did agree of my own free will."

"But I warrant you did not know what was involved."

She sighed. "One thing I did not know, and that was how guilty I would feel about Lady Ashley. I like her more than I believed possible."

"She is rather a gem," Edgar admitted.

"How did she and your mama ever become acquainted? They are sadly dissimilar."

"They may not have been in their youth. Lady Ashley and Mama were débutantes together, and became bosom friends at that time, enjoying the Season and no doubt exchanging confidences and *on dits*.

"Not long after Mama and Papa were betrothed Lady Ashley married the Earl of Ashley, who was reputed to be the richest man in England at that time. Unfortunately, Lord Ashley did not survive many years— he was a good deal older than his wife—but she has, I believe, enjoyed the fortune at her disposal. It is said she had been the mistress of many influential men, including royalty."

Amazed and impressed, Annabel answered, "I am not surprised. She is a charming lady, and I am not looking forward to her discovering who I really am."

"It is possible she will enjoy the joke hugely."

She gave him a doubtful look and he then took out his hunter, glancing at it before putting it away.

"I must be gone," he said, not without a little satisfaction. Annabel gave him a curious glance and he looked away from her. "I am to join Cranbourne and a few of his cronies."

She stiffened. "Cranbourne! Mr. Beaumont, he is not of your stamp at all. In any event, where are you going with him?"

Edgar Beaumont straightened his carefully folded neckcloth, which nestled between the two high points of his shirt collar.

"He had been exceeding condescending towards me. He has offered to take me up when I go to London for the Season, and nothing can guarantee social success more than being taken up by a member of Prinny's Carlton House Set. I shall become acquainted with Brummell and Alvanley."

His eyes grew glazed at the very thought, but Annabel was only irritated. "That may well be, but they are so much more sophisticated than you, Mr. Beaumont."

"I fail to see what that signifies. Once I take up residence in London I shall patronise tailors such as Weston, and purchase a racing curricle. I shall equal any of them, you will see."

Annabel stifled a gasp of exasperation. "I see that you will soon be parted from your allowance by Cranbourne or one of his cronies in some gambling hell in Avon Street before you even set foot in London."

Edgar smiled uncertainly. "Miss Haygarth, may I remind you that it is none of your concern? What I choose to do and with whom I do it is my concern entirely. I have long been free of leading strings. When you refused my offer of marriage you surrendered any right to have a say in what I do."

She smiled ironically. "Since when has any wife had any say in what a husband does or with whom he consorts? Your mama is a rare creature in that she does. What I tell you is for your own well-being, as a friend who is concerned for you."

The young man's face grew pink. "I am persuaded I had a fortunate escape when you refused my offer, Miss Haygarth. You are sounding like a nagging wife already. I am beginning to believe I shall remain a bachelor and retain my freedom."

When he had left the room her indulgent smile faded and after a few minutes she got her feet and hurried after him. She had just put on her bonnet when Emma came hurrying down the stairs.

"Georgia, is Mr. Beaumont here? I fancy I heard his voice."

Her eyes were so bright with expectation Annabel was sorry to have to disappoint her. "You did, but he has left now. He has many pressing engagements, I have discovered."

"Oh, Georgia, I never dreamed that your brother would be such a fine figure of a man."

"Edgar?" Annabel asked in astonishment.

"I only pray he will look upon me kindly when we are in London."

"Emma, you are very young yet. You will meet many eligible men . . ."

The girl looked at her askance. "Do you not approve of my adoration of your brother?"

Annabel's manner softened. "You are far too good for him, and I trust he will have the good sense to take advantage of your genuine affection."

The girl's face relaxed into a smile and then, drawing on her gloves, Annabel explained, "I must go out myself now, for a little while."

"Alone? Shall I call your maid to accompany you?"

"I shall be gone but a few minutes on an errand I forgot earlier. You may expect me back shortly."

She left Emma looking rather perplexed

and hurried into the street. Recalling that the marquis lodged in North Parade, Annabel began to walk in that direction, but she had only reached the Pulteney Bridge when a curricle drew up alongside her.

"Miss Beaumont, may I offer you a ride?"

She paused to look up, her heart missing a beat as he gazed down at her. His lips were curved into a smile, his eyes filled with amusement. After being arrested totally by him for a few moments, inevitably irritation overcame her.

"No, I thank you, Lord Cranbourne, but I would be obliged for a few moments of your time."

Immediately he handed the reins to his tiger and climbed down. She was still obliged to crane her neck to look into his face.

"It is an odd occurrence seeing you without Mr. Beaumont in attendance," he said as he climbed down. "For a brother and sister it is a very remarkable relationship. From my own experience, and others I have observed, they usually hate each other heartily. It is warming to see devotion which could equal that of lovers."

She stiffened. "We are a devoted family,"

she murmured and was forced to avert her eyes from his probing look.

"Miss Beaumont?" he said flicking a miniscule spot of dirt from his hessians with the riding-whip. "You wish to have words with me."

She straightened up as far as she could. "Indeed." As he quirked one eyebrow she found the courage to say, "My ... Mr. Beaumont informs me of his intention of joining you in various diversions about the town ..."

"That is so. It will be my pleasure showing your brother the many diversions Bath has to offer a young man."

"Many of which he would otherwise remain ignorant."

Unruffled by her censorious tone he agreed, "That is very possible." After a pause he ventured. "Did you merely wish to have my confirmation of what Mr. Beaumont told you?"

Irritated anew by the irony in his tone, nevertheless she went on, "Oh, Lord Cranbourne, may I appeal to your good nature, if indeed you have one? Mr. Beaumont is sadly ignorant of sophisticated society and is unequipped to game or drink with such as you."

He leaned back languidly against the curricle and regarded her from beneath lowered lids which were thickly fringed with dark lashes. After a moment, during which Annabel was acutely uncomfortable beneath his scrutiny, he scratched his cheek with the riding-whip.

"Miss Beaumont, I am not certain whether you are paying me a compliment or not."

Vexedly, she stamped her foot. "Indeed, I am not! You know very well I only wish to prevent my . . . Mr. Beaumont's ruination."

The marquis frowned at such strong words. "Surely you cannot think I would connive at such a thing," he said in shocked tones, which to Annabel's ears was insincere and mocking.

"By encouraging his participation in such pursuits as gambling and drinking to excess, you will surely do so."

"You obviously do not credit him with any sense at all."

"Oh, I see you are impossible! I knew I would be mistaken in speaking to you at all."

As she walked away he caught her arm

and drew her back towards him. When she looked at him again all traces of cynicism had gone from his manner.

"Miss Beaumont, I fully understand your concern, and it is good to see it in you, but Mr. Beaumont is quite normal in wishing to become a Corinthian, and I believe I am doing him a service in helping him achieve his ambition."

"He's nothing more than a goose-cap!"

"Although I am informed he is older than you I find it hard to believe. You are behaving much like a mother hen over one of her chicks." He released her arm at last. "Miss Beaumont, you may rest assured that no harm will come to that young man. It is true there are many who would take advantage of a young man of means, determined to prove himself a buck. You can rest assured that in my company he will sample the delights he craves, but his pocket will remain intact, so you may leave his further education safely in my hands, and in a year or so you will see him a fashionable man about town, which I am certain must please you."

After a moment's pause he added, "I trust your mind has been set at rest and you no longer accredit me with wicked intentions which do not exist."

Reluctantly she nodded, feeling confused. "Then I shall take my leave of you—for now."

He climbed back into the curricle, raised his hat to her and then drove off at a spanking pace across the bridge and out of sight.

Annabel waited a moment before beginning to walk back towards Lady Ashley's house, her feeling of bewilderment no more diminished. He was the oddest man, with such contradictions of character she could not decide whether he was a devil or a saint.

NINE

The Sydney Hotel situated at the far end of Pulteney Street was ablaze with fairy lanterns, and Lady Ashley's party could hear the music emanating from the verandah as they stepped out of her house. As the hotel was a mere few yards from the house, and the day a fine one with little breeze from the Avon, it was decided they should walk to the evening's entertainment rather than ride.

Edgar Beaumont, looking elegant in evening dress, was in an excellent mood and Annabel realised she was being foolish to worry on his behalf. He was no different to any other wealthy young man who aspired to fashionable society, and in any event it was none of her concern how he wished to spend his time and money.

"If we do not hear from your sister before long," she told him in confidential tones as they walked along the street, "I'll begin to believe I *am* Georgia Beaumont."

He gave her an amused look although he could scarce move his head for fear of spoiling the perfection of his neck-cloth. Even so he could not match the apparently effortless elegance of the man upon whom he modelled himself.

"You are far less tiresome than my sister, so I'd as lief you *were* Georgia."

"None of your funning; this is a matter of the utmost seriousness. I am very concerned."

"You need not be, as I keep assuring you, silly chit. All will be well."

Affecting a hurt attitude she replied, "You are already adopting the condescending attitude of the Cranbourne Set."

He smiled, refusing to be riled. "Annabel, I cannot understand why you have taken Cranbourne in dislike. He is such a splendid fellow with an enviable address, not to mention his tailor to whom he vouchsafes to introduce me. There is no doubting the fellow's a real top-sawyer, a true Corinthian."

Annabel cast him a wry look. "Need I like him when you are so full of his praises?"

Edgar had no chance to reply, for Emma overtook them, saying pertly, "You are not to monopolise Mr. Beaumont's company, Georgia, when you are able to avail yourself of it at any time."

"I would not dream of doing so," Annabel replied dryly.

"I hope you will engage me for one cotillion, Mr. Beaumont," Emma told him.

"It will be my pleasure, Miss Daunty."

As they walked on together Lady Ashley said, "I am bound to concede they make a handsome pair."

"Yes, I believe they do," Annabel admitted.

"I was not at all sure you would think so."

Annabel gave her a curious look. "Why do you say so?"

"Your very devotion to Edgar could well cause dissension if he became attached to another," Lady Ashley ventured.

"Our relationship is not quite what it would seem," Annabel answered in a muted voice and then added, "I can only be happy for them. They are both very young but so good-natured and full of pleasurable innocence."

Lady Ashley looked pleased. "You and Edgar are not at all alike. He is very much like his father, although not so handsome I am bound to say. Your father was a considerable catch."

Annabel had to laugh when she thought of the innocuous Mr. Beaumont, so much under the influence of his wife.

"It is difficult to envisage him thus, although I can readily believe you were all the rage of the *ton*."

The countess gave a profound sigh. "That was a long time ago, before you were even born, my dear. It doesn't do to look over one's shoulder. The present and the future is all."

Annabel did not like to be reminded of the future, for it seemed she had none to which she could reasonably look forward. However, the atmosphere at the Sydney Hotel was such to divert her uneasy thoughts for a while and she allowed herself to be amused by new acquaintances, flattered by young bucks who were obliged to accompany their mothers and alleviated the boredom of such a chore by flirting with her.

After a while she grew tired of that too and wandered into the famed gardens where there were as many people as inside the hotel. Although it was a warm evening she drew her shawl about her. Lovers wandered to and fro, laughing and whispering together while matrons and bucks paraded the walks, displaying their fine apparel for all to see and admire. Annabel had been accepted into the ranks of such society, and yet she stood outside of it, destined to be an alien for ever. She had never felt so lonely in her life before, not even when she had first found herself alone in the world with the knowledge that she would have to make her own way in life.

The fact that she had been accepted as one of the *haute monde* was a bitter-sweet experience, but it could not go on for much longer and her heart already ached with the loss. Once the pretence was over and the truth known, Lady Ashley, whom she had come to admire so much, would despise her, dear Emma would turn her back on her too, and she already looked upon the girl as a true friend. Worst of all would be the marquis's hatred of her, for the masquerade must affect him most of all if his intentions were in earnest.

She was lost in her own misery, aware that she was desperately trying not to think of Lord Cranbourne and the way he addressed her. His manner of regarding her often returned to haunt her in the lonely hours of the night, and for the very first time she began to wonder what her attitude toward him might be if she were indeed Georgia Beaumont. It was not something she had to consider very deeply; she knew in her heart she would encourage his suit and accept his offer of marriage, should he make one. As with every other heiress seeking a husband, his reason for coming up to scratch would not matter.

The realisation that the real heiress was content to marry a country curate caused her to smile to herself.

"I am giving myself airs," she told herself sternly. "Before long I shall have become too top-lofty by far."

A young buck, deep in his cups, was coming towards her and realising then that it was foolish to come alone to the gardens, she began to make her way back to the hotel from where she could still hear the music. She had walked a considerable way, she discovered; and was relieved to catch sight of Emma and Edgar just when it seemed the drunken buck was about to overtake her.

"What are you two doing out here alone?" she asked, but there was no real sternness in her manner.

"More to the point," Edgar responded, "what are *you* doing out here alone, *dear* sister?"

Annabel gave him a wry glance and Emma said, "Mr. Beaumont offered to show me the labyrinth."

Again she glanced at him. "Did he indeed? Perhaps he would be pleased to show the labyrinth to me too."

"It would be entirely proper if you came with us," Emma pointed out, obviously glad of the suggestion which, however, was not to the young man's liking.

"My sister looks all done up. I'm sure she would find it tiresome."

"How ungallant of you, Edgar," Annabel responded. "On the contrary, I have been longing to see this famous labyrinth since I arrived in Bath. Now seems to be an admirable time to explore. Supper will not be served for some time yet, and I believe Lady Ashley is occupied at present."

Edgar gave her a look of exasperation but could say no more. As they walked on Annabel whispered, "So, you were about to show Miss Daunty the labyrinth, were you? Your heart has a remarkable quality for mending, Mr. Beaumont."

"Would you have me wear the willow for ever on your behalf, Miss Haygarth?"

"Not on my account, but I have already told Miss Daunty that in my opinion she is far too good for you."

He smiled at last. "For once I am in agreement with you."

"What are you two whispering about?" Emma asked, hurrying to keep pace with them.

"My apologies, my dear," Annabel said quickly. "It is a childhood habit which we find difficult to break."

"La! How charming it is to find a brother and sister so devoted. Even though my own brother is now wed, I cannot look upon him with great affection. I recall only too well all his childhood pranks which made my life quite miserable. Did you play pranks on Georgia, Mr. Beaumont?"

"All the time," he responded in a dour tone.

They had come to the labyrinth, which many others were anxious to visit on such a fine evening.

"I assure you, Miss Daunty," Edgar told her. "it is much the same in most families, and your feelings towards your own brother are not at all unnatural."

"Does that mean that yours are?" she asked, giggling slightly.

The young man glanced at Annabel before replying, "We two have a very special relationship. Shall we venture into the maze, ladies?"

The attendant was handing out plans of the labyrinth to those who were not of a sporting turn of mind.

However, Edgar looked at it with disdain. "Using a plan is not the thing at all," he declared, and immediately pushed it into his pocket.

"Oh, Mr. Beaumont," Emma said in dismay, and then began to giggle again. "You really are very brave."

"He is exceedingly cork-brained," Annabel added and the young man cast her a dark look.

"Don't be faint-hearted, ladies. Finding one's way through a labyrinth cannot be too hard a task. Follow me and you will see how easy it is."

So saying, Edgar Beaumont led the two girls into the labyrinth. For a few minutes the way was easy to find, they soon discovered that the Sydney Gardens labyrinth was fully deserving of its reputation for being difficult as they stumbled upon several dead ends.

From the laughter and cries of dismay which could be heard from other parts of the labyrinth it was evident that many people were similarly lost. From the occasional squeals of delight it was equally clear that many did not mind being lost in there with desirable company.

"Oh, Mr. Beaumont, what shall we do?" Emma cried as they came across yet another dead end. "We have been in here an unconscionable time, and Lady Ashley will soon discover us missing. We shall never find our way out."

"I beg of you do not have the vapours, Miss Daunty. See, I have the plan here in my pocket and we shall soon find our way out."

He studied it carefully for a few moments with his two companions peering over his shoulder.

"That is all very well," Annabel reminded him, "but seeing we have not troubled to follow the plan from the outset, how do we know where we are now?"

Edgar Beaumont stroked his chin. "I fail to see the difficulty, my dear." He prodded the paper with his forefinger. " 'Tis obvious we are here."

Emma looked relieved and obviously trusted his judgment implicitly, but Annabel was not so sure.

"I am convinced we are here," she told him, pointing to another position on the plan.

"How can you possibly say so? It would be impossible for us to be anywhere near there. No, it is where I say."

"And I say not," Annabel insisted.

Emma looked uncomfortable but Edgar was evidently vexed by Annabel's argument. "Females have no notion of these matters," he said imperiously, and Annabel was beginning to understand why brothers and sisters argued endlessly. "Come, ladies, you will soon see who is correct. I shall escort you out into the Gardens again."

Obligingly Emma went to follow but Annabel said, "You will not find your way out into that direction."

He gave her an icy look. "Annabel, it has already been decided, so be pleased to come with us."

She looked at him aghast and, realising at last that he had inadvertently spoken her name, the colour drained from his cheeks.

"Why do you call her Annabel?" Emma asked in all innocence.

Edgar's lips began to open and close and it was evident he could think of no rational explanation, but then Annabel said quickly, "It is my second given name which Edgar knows full well I detest heartily so whenever he wishes to annoy me he calls me that."

It was immediately evident that the explanation was accepted without question by Emma, and Annabel's tension melted again. Edgar was evidently relieved too, for one shaking hand patted his Brutus curls in a nervous gesture.

"Georgia . . . ?"

"Oh, why will you not listen to me, Edgar?"

she responded. She waved her hand in the air. "We came from that direction, therefore," she went on waving her other hand, "it is only sense that we should go that way."

He was striving hard to control his annoyance, something he would not have done had she been his real sister.

"Will you please not argue further, my dear? It is evident you have no notion about the matter, so allow me to know what is the best direction to take."

"Oh, indeed," Emma agreed. "I am persuaded Mr. Beaumont must be correct. We must do exactly as he says."

"Just because he is a man," Annabel argued. "If I were . . . Lord Cranbourne you would be only too pleased to listen to me!"

"If you were Lord Cranbourne," Edgar responded, "I could rely upon you to talk sense, but as you are not, I have no intention of remaining here and listening to your tarradiddle any longer. Miss Daunty is growing cold."

Annabel gave a gasp of exasperation. "That is only because *you* refused to consider the plan at the outset."

Edgar firmly took hold of Emma's arm

and led her away. "Come, Miss Daunty. All this arguing is unseemly, and I'd as lief you did not witness any more of it."

"We cannot leave Georgia here alone."

"If she is so certain she knows the way out we will meet her again at the exit."

Annabel was incensed that anyone could be so stubborn and pigheaded, and certainly had no intention of following them. She immediately turned on her heel and walked in the opposite direction, determined to be at the exit long before them and prove she was correct. However, after a very few minutes, when she found herself returned to the very same spot, Annabel began to realise it was not so easy after all.

Once again, though, she sallied forth, this time in a different direction, but seemed no nearer to finding the way out on that occasion either. After wandering for what seemed to be an age she came across a couple locked in each other's arms. Startled at the encounter, of which they were not aware, she watched them for a moment or two, realising that she had never experienced such delight as these two seemed to be doing, nor was she ever likely to. All at once a feeling of loss assailed her and she hurried away, this time not caring which direction she was taking. It made no difference anyway, for she was well and truly lost.

At last she grew tired of running to and fro and found a seat where she could rest for a while. Feeling cold and miserable she sank down on to it, wondering if it was her fate to wander alone in this labyrinth for the rest of her days. It was growing dark and, accordingly, the noises from all around were lessening as people made their way back to the hotel for supper and to see the firework display.

After a while she got wearily to her feet and began her wanderings again. Having reached yet another dead end she heard footsteps approaching and turned on her heel, feeling both glad and alarmed.

"Miss Beaumont," the marquis said, experiencing, it seemed, as much surprise as she.

Annabel had never been so pleased to see anyone, but could only say, "Oh, Lord Cranbourne, I thought you must be Edgar come back to find me."

He frowned. "He surely cannot have left you here on your own."

She laughed uncertainly, feeling more

than a little foolish. "It is my own fault entirely, Lord Cranbourne. We had a little disagreement, I fear, and I was sure he had come back to see me sing small."

He smiled then, and her heart fluttered uncertainly again, for quite a different reason this time.

"I am certain he would not be so ungenerous." After a moment's pause he said hesitantly, "I trust you find him uncorrupted after carousing with me and my acquaintances."

A faint flush crept up her cheeks. "You must consider me a chuckle-head for having such foolish thoughts. Edgar is quite old enough to choose his own pursuits without help or assent from me, and the truth is I was too hasty in seeking you out."

"I hope you will never be that, Miss Beaumont."

Embarrassed, she looked away and he said, "Do you intend to await his arrival?"

"Oh no. I have languished in the place quite long enough and am ready to admit the labyrinth has defeated me."

His smile was enigmatic. "Then come with me, if indeed you wish to leave the labyrinth just now."

"Oh, indeed I do!"

He held out his hand and without hesitation she slipped hers into it. Without consulting the plan he led her through the various compartments and so sure was his step she was convinced he did know the way.

"Were you here alone with Mr. Beaumont?" he asked.

"Miss Daunty was with us, but she had the good sense to go with him."

"And Lady Ashley?"

Annabel laughed at the notion she would enter a labyrinth. "Lady Ashley is as usual in the card-room, enjoying a rubber of whist."

As if by magic they emerged into the Sydney Gardens with what seemed to be very little effort at all. She looked around her as if she could scarce believe her good fortune, and then turned to him.

"Lord Cranbourne, I am once again indebted to you."

He gazed down at her sombrely. "I trust you will not take me in dislike because of it."

She stepped back a pace. "I beg your pardon, Lord Cranbourne, but I do not understand what you mean."

"I may do you an injustice, ma'am, but I have gained the distinct impression that you have a rare independence of spirit and wish no one to aid you."

She was astounded at his perception and stiffly replied, "If I have given you that impression, Lord Cranbourne, it is an erroneous one, I assure you, and if I can in any way repay your valued assistance on several occasions I shall be only too pleased to do so."

He smiled again. "If only I could be certain you meant that."

"Be certain that I do."

"There is one way . . ."

Before she realised what he was about to do he had bent down and kissed her lightly on the lips. It lasted no more than a few seconds but long enough to send Annabel's senses reeling and turn her limbs to blancmange.

As he drew away at the last she staggered backwards, her eyes wide with shock, her sensibilities experiencing an emotion from which she felt she would never recover.

"Lord Cranbourne!"

"Consider the debt discharged, Miss Beaumont."

As he spoke she had the mad urge to tell him that she was not Georgia Beamount, but a paid companion not worthy of his attention. She had no chance to declare the truth, if indeed she would have summoned enough courage to do so, before a pitiful cry diverted both their attentions.

"Help, oh, please, someone help me."

"It would appear there is another lady in distress," the marquis remarked.

"That is Miss Daunty's voice," Annabel gasped, and then she covered her lips with her hand as laughter began to convulse her body.

"Would you have me rescue her?" he asked.

"Is anyone there who will help me?" Emma wailed again.

"Please do," Annabel urged, still trying to stifle her laughter. "I fear she must have lost faith with Edgar too."

Once again he strode into the labyrinth, to return only moments later with a rather dishevelled Emma Daunty, who was striving to regain her lost dignity.

"Lord Cranbourne, I shall be eternally in your debt," she gasped, and it was clear she had been near to tears.

Annabel waited to see if he would claim a kiss from Emma too, and at the very reminder her cheeks grew pink.

But he merely bowed, saying, "My pleasure, ma'am."

"Oh, I was so certain I would never escape. It must be a device of the devil."

"Where is Edgar?" Annabel asked at last.

The girl was wide-eyed. "I do not know. We were parted entirely by chance and I could not find him."

"Perchance Lord Cranbourne will have to sally forth in search of Edgar too."

"I will of course do so," he agreed, "although I am bound to say the pleasure cannot possibly be as great when two such charming ladies are in need of my services."

The possibility, however, was invalidated by the arrival of Edgar Beaumont himself at that moment, much to the surprise of the girls. He sauntered towards them with apparent nonchalace.

"Ah, so here you both are."

"No thanks to you," Annabel retorted.

He gave her a look of mild surprise at that rebuke but was saved the embarrassment of finding an answer, for at that moment fireworks erupted in the night sky, causing them to pause and admire the display, which was truly spectacular. It seemed the perfect climax to the evening.

After it was over they walked back towards the hotel with Annabel reflecting that the evening had turned out to be unexpectedly pleasant after all.

TEN

She awoke the following morning experiencing such euphoria that for the first time since her arrival at the spa she did not even notice that no word had arrived from Georgia Beaumont.

"I fear that something terrible must have happened," Bella complained as she prepared Annabel's morning toilette.

Annabel, however, was scarcely listening to the woman. Over and over in her mind she was busily reliving the moment the marquis had kissed her. Had it occurred only a week earlier she would have been totally outraged, but despite her euphoria she was sensible enough to know the difference between the kind of flirtatious kiss the marquis had bestowed upon her and the ones being enjoyed by several couples in the Sydney Gardens and the labyrinth.

However, such comparisons did not serve to dampen her spirits, nor did she heed the warning voices inside her own head which tried to warn her that he was a practised rake, a *beau* of the *ton* whose pride would not tolerate her indifference to him without a gallant attempt to win her heart.

"Oh, I am quite certain there is a perfectly good explanation for the silence, Bella," she answered belatedly. "If the ruse had been discovered, Lady Ashley would have been told of it by now and all would most certainly be up. The very silence indicates that there is nothing to concern us. It is like Miss Beaumont misjudged the amount of time it would take. We must not fret when even Mr. Edgar is unconcerned."

"He would be," Bella answered in grudging tones. "Begging your pardon, miss, but young men are notoriously unconcerned with all but their own pleasure."

Annabel could not argue with the wisdom of that statement and realised at last that she should be more concerned and, indeed, would be if it had not been for her enjoyment of the previous evening.

"I am at a loss what we can do, save continue to wait."

The maidservant sighed. "That is the hardest part, miss. If you are ready I shall dress you now . . ."

Edgar called round immediately after breakfast, anxious to reassure himself that neither Annabel nor Emma bore him ill-will after the events in the labyrinth.

"You need have no qualms, Mr. Beaumont. It was all my own fault for being cork-brained about so inconsequential a matter."

He looked considerably relieved and sat down at her side on the sofa. "You are so very good-natured, Miss Haygarth . . ."

She pressed one finger to her lips. "Show discretion in using that name. You know servants always eavesdrop."

Lowering his voice he answered, "I shall endeavour to remember, for I nearly caused disaster yesterday. The trouble is, my sister's name fits you ill." He moved closer to her. "It is a great mystery to me how I managed to be parted from Miss Daunty last evening. I do hope she is as forgiving as you, my dear."

"Emma Daunty is the most even-tempered creature I have ever encountered and, what is more, I'm not revealing any secrets when I say she idolises you."

He flushed slightly. "It is true I am only just beginning to be conscious of her worth, but it was to my misfortune that Cranbourne was on hand to help her. Such behaviour is like to turn a young girl's head. Do you think she is like to throw her cap over the windmill?"

"He came to my aid too," Annabel pointed out, "but my head is firmly on my shoulders this morning."

Aware of her own lie she averted her eyes from his immediately, although Edgar was not astute enough in such matters to be aware of her true feelings.

"Ah, but you are so eminently sensible, my dear."

At this Annabel laughed. "If that were so I should not be here."

For a moment there was silence between them and then he said, "Talking of Cranbourne, it seems he has been making a habit of coming to your aid of late. You must admit, surely, that he is a splendid fellow, worthy of more regard than you will allow."

"If I was to admit such sentiments," she answered sadly, "it would be to no avail. Unlike you, I do not forget who I really am—at least not too often."

The door opened and Emma Daunty came slowly in. Her rather solemn face broke into a smile of delight when she clapped eyes on their visitor.

"Mr. Beaumont, I had no notion you were here."

He rose quickly to his feet. "I came in the hope of seeing you."

Her cheeks grew pink and he went on, "I wished to make sure you were fully recovered from your ordeal of being lost in the labyrinth."

Breathlessly she answered, glancing excitedly at Annabel, "You make too much of it. You have no cause for concern on my part. I'm persuaded Georgia was in far more distress—at least until Lord Cranbourne arrived."

He smiled happily at Annabel too. "Then, perchance, my dear Miss Daunty, you would be kind enough to reserve several sets for me at the ball at the Assembly Room this evening."

The color in Emma's cheeks grew even deeper. "It will be my pleasure, Mr. Beaumont."

The young man pulled at his waistcoat as he gave Annabel another satisfied smile. "Excellent. I am the most fortunate of men and I shall now take my leave of you until this evening."

"You seem in something of a hurry," Annabel ventured.

He looked a little abashed. "One of my horses has turned into something of a daisy cutter, so I am taking advantage of Cranbourne's offer to find me another, and as he is such a good judge of horseflesh it would be foolish of me to miss the opportunity. Until this evening, ladies . . ."

Emma watched him go and then with eyes that shone excitedly she turned to Annabel. "Oh, is he not the most splendid fellow you have ever met?"

Wryly Annabel answered, "He is tolerably well presented, I fancy."

Emma giggled bashfully and then said, "Aunt Phoebe sent me to tell you she is ready to go out now."

Annabel was immediately on her feet. She did not find visits to the Pump Room particularly diverting, especially today when it was clear she would not see Lord Cranbourne there, but all the same she answered, "I shall fetch my hat and pelisse."

As she went up the stairs she was slightly troubled, for it was evident that Edgar and Emma were becoming more than a little attached to each other. That in itself did not trouble her, for they were a well-matched couple, and in other circumstances she would have been delighted. However, she was uneasily aware that once her own duplicity was uncovered and Edgar's part in covering up his sister's elopement revealed, Lady Ashley might wish to discourage her niece's attachment. Annabel did not think Lady Ashley was in the least a vindictive person, but she really had no notion how the woman would react to the discovery of how thoroughly she had been duped. After that Annabel was certain the countess would not look favourably upon anything which Edgar did.

If it did come about that these two young people had their happiness shattered because of Georgia's elopement, Annabel considered it would be a tragedy, but could see no way of avoiding it.

The rest of the day passed in the usual pleasant way. Somewhat philosophically Annabel had decided that as she was powerless to intervene she would allow events to take their natural course. The return of her euphoria perhaps had some bearing on her recollection that the evening brought the prospect of a meeting with the marquis again, for he was certain to be at the ball being held at the Upper Assembly Rooms. Her heart beat unevenly at the very thought. Every moment with him would be a stolen one, but something to recall with pleasure during the uncertain days ahead.

Bella had become very silent, which irked Annabel no less than her habitual worrying out loud. She still dutifully laid out Annabel's outfits for each occasion, and, as a consequence of her efforts, the girl was always perfectly attired.

As the maidservant dressed Annabel's hair in a becoming confusion of curls she ventured, "Bella, have you ever paused to consider what will become of you if Mrs. Beaumont dismisses you for your part in this escapade?"

Bella's deft fingers paused. "Miss Georgia will be Mrs. Quinton and then I will serve her again in her new station in life."

"Ah, but what if something goes wrong during the elopement and Miss Beaumont does not become Mrs. Quinton after all?"

"I am convinced that nothing will go amiss with their plans at this late moment, but if it does happen I shall be obliged to face the world on my own, miss. It cannot be helped. Mrs. Beaumont would not have me beneath her roof after this, and those of us who serve are always at the whims of our masters."

Annabel was moved at such a stoic acceptance of circumstances which were often cruel and unfair. She herself was in very much the same position, although she had in the earlier part of her life, experienced a more privileged existence, which was why subservience fitted her ill. At that moment she almost envied Bella's acceptance of her role in life. There was no conflict in her mind, which was more than Annabel could admit to.

"You are very loyal, Bella. Miss Beaumont is fortunate in having you serve her."

"I'm devoted to her, miss, so my part in this is inevitable. I'll always do her bidding and she knows it. It is you who is deserving of admiration."

Suddenly her fingers faltered and Annabel gave her a curious look to find the servant staring out of the window.

"What is it, Bella?"

"You'd bèst take a look for yourself, Miss."

Annabel got slowly to her feet, feeling curious now. She walked to the window which overlooked Pulteney Street. A travelling chaise had pulled up outside the house, the team of horses sweating profusely. Lady Ashley's footman had put down the steps and just as Annabel glanced out of the window none other than Mrs. Beaumont climbed down, causing the girl at the window almost to choke in alarm.

Mrs. Beaumont never ventured from Hetherington Howard, and yet here she was, warmly dressed for travelling and looking as robust as Annabel had always believed her to be. She gasped out loud and withdrew from the window, flattening herself against the wall for fear that she would be seen.

Her eyes were wide with fear. "All is up now! Mrs. Beaumont is here."

"Who'd have thought she would make the journey?"

Annabel cast her a desperate look. " 'Tis obvious news of Miss Beaumont's elopement has reached her, but why have we not heard? I assumed we should hear of the successful elopement first from Miss Beaumont herself, which would have given us enough time to move on before discovery. What are we to do now? In a matter of minutes Lady Ashley will know all and wonder who she has harboured these past two weeks and more."

There came a knock at the door. Annabel and the maid-servant exchanged anxious looks before Annabel drew a deep breath and went to open the door herself.

To her surprise it was the countess who stood there. She was already dressed for dinner but her face was unusually strained as, Annabel suspected, was her own.

"May I come in?"

She opened the door wider to allow her in. At the same time Bella started to go, but Lady Ashley waved to her.

"You may as well remain, Bella."

"Lady Ashley . . ." Annabel began although, in truth, she did not know what to say.

The countess walked across the room, her bejewelled fingers clasped tightly together. "We have no time to prevaricate, my dear. Ada Beaumont waits below and I cannot delay her for long." She turned on her heel. "In truth, I do not know what has brought her here, for she comes unheralded, although I can hazard a guess what the matter concerns.

"What is most important now is for you to remain here in this room and not come down until I give you leave. It would not do for her to see you."

She began to leave the room whilst Annabel looked at her in astonishment. "Lady Ashley, you know about me already, don't you?"

At last the woman's face broke into a smile. "Yes, my dear, I know."

"How . . . how long?"

"Why, from the moment you arrived, of course."

As Bella clasped her hands to her lips and Annabel remained rigid with shock Lady Ashley drew out a small painted miniature which she held so Annabel could see it. The face of Georgia Beaumont stared back her, as unlike her own as could be.

"Ada Beaumont is, if nothing else, an astute woman. Knowing I am both wealthy and childless she has made certain I was always kept up to date over the years with matters concerning my godchild. This miniature arrived less than a twelve month ago. I could not believe she had changed so much."

Annabel's head was reeling with the shock she had been dealt. "Why on earth did you not denounce me from the outset?"

Lady Ashley sank down on to the day-bed, still clutching the miniature. "You arrived in the Beaumont carriage with Georgia's maid and all her clothes, so naturally I was curious. I came to Bath to recover from an illness but I have long recovered from it and of late life has grown tedious. I decided to remain silent and see what transpired in the hope that it might divert me. I confess that it has. My knowledge of human nature told me you were no villainess, and that there must be a good reason for your being here in Georgia's shoes.

"Ada has kept me informed of all that transpired at Hetherington Howard, including her daughter's reluctance to come to Bath because of an attachment to a Mr. Quinton. As you know, I also had a graphic description of Edgar's infatuation for her ungrateful companion."

Annabel averted her eyes and Lady Ashley added, "I could not be certain of anything, so on your first day I took the liberty of having my maid search your belongings. She found several volumes of poetry inscribed with the name of Annabel Haygarth . . ."

Annabel shook her head in bewilderment. "I can scarce believe this. Do you not realise if you had denounced me when I arrived you might have been able to avert the elopement?"

It was the countess's turn to look bewildered. "Why should I wish to do that? I found the entire business hugely diverting, for I had no notion Georgia was so resourceful. To defy Ada Beaumont in such a way seemed miraculous to me. When I ascertained you were the disgraced companion I immediately dispatched a note to my old friend, suggesting Edgar should join us."

Annabel was plainly incredulous. "You are veritable mischiefmaker, Lady Ashley. I cannot credit it in you."

The woman smiled wryly. "It is obvious you think me a wicked woman, my dear. I have no defence for what I did."

"I cannot condemn you, my lady."

"Tush. You acted out of the goodness of your heart, not from some dark wish to settle an old score."

Annabel gave her a curious look and she went on in a quiet voice. "Revenge might not be too dramatic a word to use." After a moment's pause Lady Ashley went on, "You may already know Ada and I made our débuts together twenty years ago. Not long after I came out into society I fell in love and sensed he was a man I could love to the end of my life. I had high hopes that he would come up to scratch and no one could have been happier." She drew a deep sigh. "That man was George Beaumont. Ada also decided she must have him and although I will spare you the details of the rivalry which ensued that Season it is enough that at last she was the one triumphant. Not long afterwards I became betrothed to Ashley, who had made it plain since my début that he loved me and wished me to be his wife. He was older than me and I did not love him. I could not love him. To his credit

Ashley knew that, but he was satisfied and I do not believe I was a bad wife to him."

There was a moment's pause, during which the silence was heavy, and then Annabel said in a choked voice, "Lady Ashley, I quite understand, but there was no need for you to pain yourself . . ."

"You have a kind heart, but please don't pity me, my dear. My marriage was a happy one for all its beginnings. Ashley was a kind and indulgent husband. Since then I have known much happiness but the chance to be revenged at last upon Ada Beaumont— and indeed to ensure she did not ruin her children's chance of happiness as she almost did to mine was too much to resist. Initially, keeping quiet so that Georgia could marry the man of her choice was all that I intended to do, but," she added, grinning engagingly, "I did hope to see Edgar settled with Ada's paid companion. That would have been recompense in great measure."

"Oh, no, Lady Ashley . . ."

"Once I saw you together I did realise you were not at all suited and Ada may well see him, after all, leg-shackled to a considerable heiress—my niece. They are a pleasant enough pair and I would not see them unhappy for the world, so on that score I can do nothing. However, if there was no possibility of your marrying Edgar, seeing the disgraced companion elevated to the position of countess would really have had her on the raws." She looked at Annabel consideringly. "I still have hopes that it may come to pass, although for your sake rather than my wicked one."

At this pronouncement Annabel became agitated. "That is out of the question, Lady Ashley. He believes me to be Georgia Beaumont, otherwise he would not give me a moment of his time."

The countess shrugged slightly and got to her feet. "I must go and face my old friend, and think up what excuse I may for confirming the arrival of my goddaughter."

However, it was Annabel who reached the door first. "That I cannot agree. Allow me to go in your stead. I owe you at least such a service."

The woman smiled yet again. "You owe me nothing, and Ada Beaumont is like to eat you up alive. You have already demonstrated that you are brave to a sufficient degree. Facing her now would solve nothing." She gave her another considering look. "You didn't falter once, you know."

Annabel laughed. "I did on many an occasion, and was tempted to do so on even more. I did not," she added, "enjoy lying to you."

"You have a stout heart and a romantic mind, which is more than can be said of Ada Beaumont, who has a blacksmith's anvil where her heart should be and an abacus for a mind."

When she had gone Bella said with satisfaction, "So it seems Miss Georgia has succeeded after all."

"Mrs. Beaumont must have set out immediately she heard. She will wish to know why Lady Ashley wrote to say Miss Beaumont had arrived when it is patently obvious she has been in Gretna a fortnight, although why she has seen fit to endure the rigours of the journey I cannot conceive." She glanced quickly around the room, adding, "In any event I had best put together what few belongings I have with me."

"Don't act hastily, miss. I have the feeling Lady Ashley will not wish you to go."

Annabel looked up at her for a moment as she began to put her personal belongings in a cloak-bag. She supposed there was a great deal of truth in what Bella suggested and it was an attractive proposition in many ways. Only the thought of meeting the marquis with the truth exposed decided her against such a possibility.

At last she answered, "Nevertheless, I shall not impose upon her further." She glanced at the abigail and smiled. "You have served your mistress well, Bella. She will be well pleased with you."

"Let me help you pack your things, miss."

Annabel laughed. "There is little enough, but I have only Miss Beaumont's clothes to wear, so if you will be so good as to tell her I shall return her travelling gown as soon as I am able."

"I am certain Miss Georgia would want you to have it."

Annabel smiled warily. "Well, all that remains is for me to bid goodbye to Lady Ashley which I shall do in a note." She hesitated. "It will be best if I am gone quickly, before Mrs. Beaumont has any chance to see me. That can only increase her wrath."

"But what will you do, Miss? Where will you go?"

"Just what I intended before Miss Beaumont involved me in her elopement. The intervening two weeks has been a pleasant interlude, Bella; I cannot admit to anything else. It has been a fine experience living as a lady."

As she spoke Annabel suddenly realised that not only would she be bidding goodbye to Lady Ashley and Emma, but she was never likely to see the marquis again. His warm smile or his quizzical glance was lost to her for ever.

That was the one thought which caused her infinite pain.

ELEVEN

"You really should wait until you have spoken to Lady Ashley," Bella begged of Annabel as she watched her fasten her fur-trimmed pelisse. "She will be angry with me if you go without speaking with her first."

"I have made up my mind, Bella, that it is better I go now. I am no longer afraid of Mrs. Beaumont but if she discovers me here it will go worse for Lady Ashley. Please see that she gets this note."

"I will, miss, and I'll tell Miss Georgia that you've done her proud."

Annabel smiled faintly, taking up her cloak-bag. "Good luck, Bella. I hope you find your mistress well and happy, and pray tell her I shall be applying to her for a recommendation when one is needed."

"I will, and good luck to *you*, miss."

Annabel hurried down the stairs. Oddly enough, she felt no relief at the pretence being over at last. Instead, she experienced only sadness, hating to leave these people to whom she had become so much attached.

Outside Lady Ashley's drawing-room one of the footmen was straining his ears to hear what was going on within and when Annabel appeared he jumped to attention. There really was no need for him to eavesdrop, however, for Mrs. Beaumont's voice was sufficiently loud for them to hear with ease.

"Ten whole days she has lain ill at some wretched inn in Carlisle!" Mrs. Beaumont exclaimed. "And all the while we believed her safe in Bath. *You* told me she had arrived safely."

"Really, Ada, you must not apportion blame to me. I have not seen the chit since she was on leading strings. I was so certain it was she."

"Then there is someone here in Georgia's stead?"

"Naturally. Why else would I inform you of her safe arrival?"

"Who is it masquerading as my child?"

"Do you not know?" Lady Ashley asked, and there was a wealth of innocence in her voice.

"I am beginning to have a notion, but no . . . it could not be. It is not possible . . . Let us call the watch and have her arrested."

"Let us not be so rash. No one has broken any laws and, besides, Georgia is safe, is she not?"

"No thanks to that poltroon whom I will now be forced to acknowledge as my son-in-law. In the circumstances, all will know of the elopement. We will be the laughing stock of the county. Oh, it really is too bad! I had such plans for her. She could have been a duchess."

"It is better that she is happy," the countess pointed out in a gentle tone."

"You are a fool, Phoebe."

"And so are you. There are some people who truly know their own minds, and Georgia is one of them. In that she favours you, Ada."

"I was never so foolish, and if you had any wits about you I would have been able to stop this nonsense at the outset. What I have come to discover is what part you had in this abominable business."

Lady Ashley laughed. "I am an innocent pawn in this affair, my dear. Your daughter did not deem to inform me that she intended to elope."

"And if she had I wager you would have aided her."

"Perhaps I would. It is true I did not *know* she had eloped, I see no reason why I should not confess that Georgia wrote to me some weeks ago and confided her unhappiness over Mr. Quinton, who seemed to be an admirable young man, able to control your daughter's more cork-brained notions. I did advise her to elope, but in truth I never imagined your daughter would have retained sufficient spirit actually to do so."

Mrs. Beaumont gasped. "You are really beyond all reason, Phoebe. It is obvious I shall receive no help or sympathy from you, although I cannot conceive what I have done to earn such treatment from one I looked upon as a sister."

Annabel began to move towards the landing as Lady Ashley said soothingly, "Oh, do stay, my dear. After a night's rest you are bound to see that all is not so bleak."

"I would not dream of remaining beneath your roof a moment longer. Indeed, I turn my back on you for good. My priority now is to see my son and discover his part in this, not to mention ascertaining what manner of evil has befallen him in this foul place."

Just as Annabel reached the first step the door to Lady Ashley's drawing-room opened and Mrs. Beaumont came bursting out with the countess hovering behind. Mrs. Beaumont's eyes were bright, her cheeks full of colour, but when she caught sight of Annabel her face almost turned purple.

"You! What are you doing here?"

"This is the young lady I believed to be Georgia," Lady Ashley explained.

"Oh, really! That is too much, but I suspected you might be involved in this mischief." She turned to her erstwhile friend. "You took *this* miserable creature for my daughter, this *servant*?"

"She has very pretty manners, Ada."

Lady Ashley's tone was of such innocence Annabel was almost tempted to laugh.

"This is the viper I took to my bosom, and see how she has repaid my kindness. Is there no end to the evil she has perpetrated against me and my family?"

"Ada, you have caused this mayhem by your own unreasonable behaviour," the countess told her, not unkindly. "You were never reasonable."

Annabel thought Mrs. Beaumont might burst. "If I were a man I would call you out." She looked at Annabel again. "I suppose I must be thankful you didn't persuade my son to elope with *you*."

"She has not had the opportunity," Lady Ashley answered. "The Marquis of Cranbourne has been paying court to her ever since she arrived and even had he wished to do so too, dear Edgar had little chance."

Of course, Lady Ashley knew just what she was saying and the result of her pronouncement could scarcely have pleased her more. Mrs. Beaumont's face grew dark with impotent fury and she clutched at her heart with her hand. Annabel was truly afraid she might succumb to a seizure, and Lady Ashley was concerned too.

"Ada, my dear, you look positively queer. It must be the journey which has done you up. Allow me to burn feathers for you. It is the least I can do."

Looking no less angry the woman swept past them both and giving Annabel a look which would freeze water, she hurried down the stairs and out of the house.

As the carriage drove away at a spanking pace and the footman closed the door a profound silence descended upon the house until Lady Ashley drew a sigh. Whether it was one of satisfaction or just relief Annabel could not tell.

After a moment the countess gave her an appraising look. "You should have remained upstairs."

"Is it true Miss Beaumont is married?"

"They wed at Gretna as arranged but on that very night Georgia took ill with a fever and they could travel no farther. Physicians fees and the inn charges soon emptied Mr. Quinton's purse and finally he was obliged to inform the Beaumonts. Happily, she is well recovered and there is little the Beaumonts can or will do now, save give their blessing."

"I am glad about that at least. It is poor Edgar I pity now. Mrs. Beaumont will really give him a setdown for his part in this."

"Let us hope some of her choler will have abated a little by the time she finds him.

Prudently, I wrote a note to him just before I went to face his mother. If he has a small amount of sense I credit him with, he will absent himself from his lodgings for a while."

She gave Annabel a sharp look then. "Where do you think you are going at this time of the day?"

"It is best if I go now, Lady Ashley."

"I don't agree. There is no longer any cause for you to go and you are most welcome to remain here with me."

Annabel shook her head. "You are very kind, but by the morrow the story will be known all over Bath."

"That doesn't concern me in the least, but I can recognise why it might trouble you. There is someone you would as lief not face."

Annabel averted her eyes and Lady Ashley went on in a brisk tone of voice, "Where will you go?"

"I have not yet decided. It would be best if I just leave."

Lady Ashley watched her thoughtfully and when Annabel finished speaking she ordered, "Wait here. The least I can do is provide some money to tide you over, and when you are settled you must let me know."

She hurried back into the drawing-room as Annabel began to protest, and the moment she had gone Annabel picked up her cloak-bag, hurrying down the stairs and out into the night before the countess could return. Her eyes were blurred with tears as she hurried along Pulteney Street, so much so that she bumped into several people on her way. She only hoped that she would not encounter anyone she knew, for that would be too humiliating.

After crossing the Pulteney Bridge she looked around in vain for a sedan chair, but as so many people were making their way to the Assembly Rooms none was available. Eventually, she gave up trying to find one and began to walk towards the staging inn, where she would purchase a ticket on the first London-bound stage out of Bath.

By the time she reached the inn she was tired, although emotion had robbed her, it seemed, of her appetite, and she was hardly aware of missing dinner.

Arriving on foot, carrying her own cloak-bag, Annabel did not present a very important figure although her clothes and manner identified her a lady. Rubbing his hands together, the landlord eyed her curiously, understandably unable to decide whether she merited his personal attention or not.

"What'll be your pleasure, ma'am?"

She handed him her cloak-bag. "What time does the next coach to London leave here?"

"Six o'the clock on the morrow, ma'am."

She was taken aback, but quickly recovered her surprise. "Then I shall wait if I may."

"With pleasure, ma'am." He stroked his chin, still unsure of her status. "A private parlour is available."

Mentally, she made a reckoning of her resources and after a pause answered, "That will not be necessary, landlord."

His manner then became a mite less obsequious. "In here, then, ma'am."

He led her along a stone-flagged corridor, past rooms filled with carousing bucks. He flung open a door at the end of the corridor and ushered her into a room which was already crowded. It seemed she was not the only one who awaited a stagecoach out of the town, and those awaiting looked at her curiously as she slowly walked around. Because she did not like the way the gentlemen were eyeing her she seated herself on a bench between a thin but respectable-looking woman and another nursing a young child on her knee. The men continued to eye her appreciatively and Annabel rewarded them with icy looks.

For a while she sat rigidly in the seat, unaware of the discomfort of the hard bench. Time passed slowly and eventually she was able to doze, which was far preferable to being alone with her thoughts. Although she knew she had never truly possessed Lord Cranbourne's regard—she had no right to it—nevertheless the sense of loss she experienced was deep, gnawing at her heart. Even Georgia Beaumont had fallen in love with a man beneath her station, how ridiculous it was that she, Annabel Haygarth, should fall in love with a man so far above her.

The door opened again, causing her head to jerk upwards. The landlord was bowing low before a man, who swept him to one side with a solitary move of his arm. He strode into the room, attracting the attention of all who waited. He was wearing evening dress, so that even if he had not invited interest by his very presence, his appearance would have done so.

Annabel was immediately awake and she shrank back, but the marquis's glance raked the room. His eyes narrowed slightly when they caught sight of her.

"So here you are."

Once again her eyes brimmed with tears as she averted her face. "Why, oh why, did you come? Please go away and let me be."

It was as if she had never spoken, for he came across the room and, taking her by the arm, drew her to her feet. For a moment he just gazed at her and she could not move, a prisoner of that dark and probing look. Then he began to guide her across the room, to the amusement of the other travellers, who started to talk excitedly among themselves. No one made a move to stop him, even though it must have been evident to them that she didn't wish to accompany this man.

"Unhand me, Lord Cranbourne," she hissed, trying to free herself, but he kept a firm hold on her until they had reached a private parlour.

"You go too far!" she cried as he kicked the door closed behind them.

He pushed her into a chair and then, going over to the fireplace, he put one foot on the grate.

"How on earth did you find me?" she asked wearily.

"Lady Ashley had the good sense to send a message to my lodgings, informing me of your flight. Fortunately, I had not yet left. It so happened that Edgar Beaumont had come to me with shaking knees to crave advice on learning his mother had arrived in town, so I was already acquainted with some of the facts of the matter."

"Poor Edgar," she murmured.

"I have left him there to cool his heels."

"I do not envy him when she finds him at last."

"He will behave as any man should, you can be sure. In any event," he added wryly, "she can do nothing but berate him, although from all I have heard, that will be bad enough."

Annabel pushed back a renegade lock of hair and he added, not unkindly, "What a tangled web. I'll wager you did not consider the matter would grow so complicated when you set out on this lark."

"It was no lark, but I'm persuaded that nothing can be gained by a discussion on the subject now."

"You are quite correct, my dear. I wish to

discuss quite a different matter with you; the matter of our marriage . . ."

From wallowing in her own misery Annabel looked up at him in alarm. "Lord Cranbourne!"

He smiled. "In view of what I have just said, you may call me Philip."

She began to laugh and he said in hurt tones, "Do you find my name so amusing?"

She shook her head. "I fear that Lady Ashley and Mr. Beaumont only omitted to tell you I am not Georgia Beaumont. My name is Annabel Haygarth and I am a penniless orphan who is normally employed as a paid companion. I was with Mrs. Beaumont until she dismissed me for allegedly seducing her son. I did no such thing but justice is not a word with which Mrs. Beaumont is acquainted."

He moved across the room and seated himself in a chair which faced hers. "You must think I'm not up to snuff. Of course I know you are not Georgia Beaumont even though you could humble a duchess with your manner. What is more, my dearest girl, I have known it from the outset."

Annabel's eyes widened with surprise and then she started to laugh again and continued to laugh until tears began to stream down her cheeks. Lord Cranbourne watched her indulgently for a few moments before he handed her a cambric handkerchief with which she wiped her cheeks.

"Georgia Beaumont thought it such a ingenious idea," she gasped.

"She was always a foolish chit."

She looked at him. "You must have recalled her very well after all."

"Oh, immediately I caught sight of her at the Black Swan. She was such a tiresome child, the moment I clapped eyes on her I determined to avoid her.

"She did not recall *you*."

He smiled. "Ah, vanity. In any event I did become interested in Miss Beaumont's travelling companion, who was far more to my fancy." Her cheeks grew pink as he went on, "So I tipped the landlord a substantial vail to tell me her name. Miss Beaumont, he told me, was travelling with a Miss Haygarth. I saw Miss Beaumont drive away from the inn with a young gentleman, which I considered odd as I had been informed that she was bound for Bath. However, I didn't truly begin to be intrigued until the incident on Coombe Down when the lady whom I knew to be Miss Haygarth was introduced to me as Miss Beaumont and continued to be Miss Beaumont when she arrived in Bath. As soon as I was able, I sought out the company of Lady Ashley, who was obliging enough to confide that she hadn't set eyes upon her goddaughter for some sixteen years . . ."

Annabel shook her head. "Lady Ashley knew I wasn't Georgia; you knew. It was all for nothing."

"I would not say that." He gazed at her and she looked away. "What truly concerns me is your real relationship with Edgar Beaumont. If he is not your brother . . ."

Quickly she looked up again. "Oh, Philip, he is not my lover. He merely gave me a helping hand for the fun of it. He thought it a great lark.

"Lady Ashley went along with the pretence for revenge, you know, and I . . ." She sighed. "I am glad Georgia Beaumont has achieved her heart's desire, but I must confess I was moved to come to Bath out of a desire to settle the account with Mrs. Beaumont. There, you now know what a wicked creature I am."

Jumping to his feet he laughed, much to

her alarm, before sweeping her to her feet and into his arms.

"If you are a wicked woman, I adore you for it!"

So saying, he kissed her with more thoroughness than before and she had no wish to draw away. It seemed as though she had belonged in his arms for ever.

At last she did draw away from him, saying shyly, "Do you truly not mind my not being an heiress?"

"You, my dear, possess far greater riches than mere money, and I would be a fool if I were not conscious of it."

Once again she relaxed against his shoulder. "I fear, however, that there will be a great deal of tattle when your intentions become known, and Mrs. Beaumont is certain to make mischief where she can."

"You will have far more influential people to champion you than Mrs. Beaumont. Brummell will adore you and no one, not even the Prince of Wales himself, dares to gainsay the Beau; and once you are my wife no one will care who you were before that." He held her away. "It seems every one has emerged from this escapade the happier."

"Save Mrs. Beaumont!"

"No doubt she will feel more content when her elder son allies himself to one of the richest heiresses in England—as I am certain he will."

"Miss Daunty?" Annabel asked in surprise.

"Yes, Miss Daunty," he answered, evidently amused by her astonishment.

"I was aware she had a portion but . . ."

"It is to Mr. Beaumont's credit that he is probably unaware of it too, but you can be sure his mother will know of the Dauntys."

"They are a delightful pair, but I don't think Mrs. Beaumont deserves such good fortune."

He gathered her close in his arms again. "Ah, but just think of her fury when she learns that you are to marry me."

Cradled in his arms she did consider it briefly and she was surprised to discover that she didn't really care what Mrs. Beaumont might think, for the notion gave *her* a great deal of pleasure.